Oliver Optic

On Time

Or, the Young Captain of the Ucayga Steamer

Oliver Optic

On Time
Or, the Young Captain of the Ucayga Steamer

ISBN/EAN: 9783337184469

Printed in Europe, USA, Canada, Australia, Japan

Cover: Foto ©Andreas Hilbeck / pixelio.de

More available books at **www.hansebooks.com**

LAKE SHORE SERIES.

BY

OLIVER OPTIC.

ON TIME.

LEE & SHEPARD.
BOSTON.

THE LAKE SHORE SERIES.

ON TIME

OR,

THE YOUNG CAPTAIN

OF THE

UCAYGA STEAMER.

BY

OLIVER OPTIC,

Author of "Army and Navy Stories," "Great Western Series," "Onward and Upward Stories," "Woodville Stories," Famous "Boat-Club Series," "The Starry-Flag Series," "Young America Abroad," "Lake-Shore Series," "Riverdale Story-Book," "Yacht-Club Series," and "The Boat-Builder Series."

BOSTON:
LEE AND SHEPARD, PUBLISHERS.
NEW YORK:
CHARLES T. DILLINGHAM.

ELECTROTYPED AT THE
BOSTON STEREOTYPE FOUNDRY,
NO. 19 SPRING LANE.

TO

MY YOUNG FRIEND

SIGOURNEY BUTLER

𝔗𝔥𝔦𝔰 𝔅𝔬𝔬𝔨

IS AFFECTIONATELY DEDICATED.

THE LAKE SHORE SERIES.

PREFACE.

"ON TIME" is the third of THE LAKE SHORE SERIES, and, like its predecessors, has appeared as a serial in Oliver Optic's Magazine. The author is pleased to know, as he has learned from hundreds of letters from Our Boys and Girls, that Wolf Penniman, the hero of the story, is a general favorite. He is entirely willing to acknowledge that the young captain is a smart boy; that he does great things for a young man of his years; and that he brings about results which, while they are not inconsistent with the record of history, are grand achievements for one of his age. Boys of sixteen are not babies nowadays, and they expect their heroes to be wide-awake, live young men.

The writer has endeavored, in these pages, to illustrate the blessed precept, "Love your enemies," and to convince his young friends that a wide-awake boy may have the principles of the gospel in his heart, and may carry them into practice in his daily life.

HARRISON SQUARE, MASS.,
July 21, 1869.

CONTENTS.

ON TIME;

OR,

THE YOUNG CAPTAIN OF THE UCAYGA STEAMER.

CHAPTER I.

A NEW PROJECT.

"YOU don't want that boat, Wolf, any more than the lake wants water," said my father, after I had read an advertisement, in the Ruoara Clarion, of the effects of a bankrupt which were to be sold at auction the next day.

"I don't think the lake would amount to much without water; in fact, to no more than I do without business," I replied. "I want something to do, and if I can buy this boat at a low price, I am sure I can make something out of her."

"What can you do with her? She is a very pretty

plaything; but you and I can't afford such luxuries," added my father.

"I don't want her for a plaything, father," I persisted. "I want to make some money out of her."

"You are an enterprising boy, Wolf; but I really don't see any money in a boat like that."

"I think there is, though of course I may be mistaken. Since Major Toppleton has been running his steamers across the lake to Centreport so many times a day, the ferry would not pay, and the owner has gone up to Ruoara with his boat. Now, there are many people who wish to cross between the steamers' trips."

"I don't think that would pay," said my father, shaking his head.

"There is hardly a boat to let, either in Middleport or Centreport. I think a boat kept for parties of pleasure would pay well. There are plenty of people who want to go up the lake fishing; and there would be a great many more if a decent boat were to be had."

"Well, Wolf, you have made your own money, and you are smart enough to take care of it yourself. If you want to go into a speculation on your own account, I haven't a word to say. But what will this boat cost?"

"Of course I don't mean to pay anything like her value. If she can be bought at a low figure, I can do something with her, even if I have to sell her."

"They say she cost five or six hundred dollars."

"I should say she could not be built and fitted up for anything less than six hundred. I am willing to go one hundred on her. If I can buy her for that, I can turn her again so as to double my money," I continued, confidently.

"I don't know. A boat is either the best or the worst property in the world."

"I know that. It is October now, and the boating season is about over, though there is considerable fishing done up the lake. Not many people want to buy a boat in the fall, and for that reason she won't bring much."

"Here is the hundred dollars. If you can buy her for that, I think you will be safe enough," added my father, as he took the bills from the bureau drawer.

I was very fond of boating, and would rather have made my living in that way than any other; but while I could get two, or even one dollar a day for running an engine, I could not afford to risk my chances with a boat. I was out of business now. I had been contemptuously discharged from the Lake Shore Railroad, and, not a little to my chagrin, Colonel Wimpleton, who had made me liberal offers to serve in his new steamer, did not repeat them. My father also was out of employ, and, though we were not likely to suffer at present for the want of work, we could ill afford to be idle.

I had taken it into my head that I could make something with a good sail-boat. The people of the two towns, as well as many strangers who came to them, were fond of fishing, and six or seven dollars a day for such a boat as I proposed to buy would not be an extravagant price, including, as it would, my own services as skipper. Twenty days' work would refund my capital, and I could reasonably hope to obtain this amount of business during the next two months. The next summer she would be a small fortune to me, for boats were in constant demand.

The next day I crossed the lake, and went up to Ruoara in Colonel Wimpleton's new steamer, the Ucayga. This was the first time I had sailed in her, and I could not help seeing that she was " a big thing." It seemed almost incredible to me that I had been offered the situation of captain of this boat, and even more incredible that I had refused it; but both of these statements were true. I had come to the conclusion that the colonel had repented of his splendid offer.

Just now the Lake Shore Railroad was in the ascendant, and the Ucayga was under a shadow. She had very few passengers, while the train which had just left Middleport had been crowded. It was a busy season among travellers, and I heard that the colonel was terribly galled by the ill success of his line. Major Toppleton had ordered the captains of the two boats which ran up the lake to be regularly ten minutes behind time, so that the steamer was unable to leave Centreport in season to connect with the trains at Ucayga. This delay entirely defeated the colonel's plans, and the Ucayga was generally obliged to leave without any of the through passengers, which comprised more than half the travel. Without them the boat would not pay.

It did not make much difference to Colonel Wimpleton whether the steamer made or lost money for him, if he could only get ahead of the railroad. The Ucayga had failed to connect with the railroads at the foot of the lake two or three times a week; and this had given her a very bad reputation. It was true that the Lightning Express, on which I had formerly run as engineer, had been similarly unfortunate quite a number of times; but as the major's plan was fully understood by the people up the lake, the train was regarded as the surer of the two modes of conveyance.

Lewis Holgate, the son of the man who had robbed my father, was still the engineer of the Lightning Express. He was under the powerful protection of Tommy Toppleton, who ruled all Middleport by ruling his father, the magnate of the town. Lewis was a treacherous wretch. He had labored to ruin me, under the direction of his young master; but I tried to think as kindly of him as I could. I was daily in fear that, through his unskilful management of the locomotive, an accident would occur on the road. I am almost sure that Colonel Wimpleton would have hailed such a catastrophe with satisfaction, so deep and bitter was his hatred of Major Toppleton, and so great was his opposition to the road. As the matter stood, neither the train nor the steamer was entirely reliable. A little more shrewdness, skill, and enterprise would have turned the scale in favor of either.

The Ucayga started this morning without waiting for the arrival of the up-lake steamer. As soon as she left the wharf, I began to walk about her decks and cabins on an exploring tour. I was delighted with her appointments; and, while I tried to be impartial between the steamer and the railroad, my admiration of the beautiful craft inclined me to believe that she ought to win. In the course of my wanderings about the boat, I came to the forward deck. About the first person I encountered here was Mr. Waddie Wimpleton. He sat on the capstan, smoking a cigar, for the young scion of the Wimpleton house was bent on being as "big" as anybody else.

"What are you doing on our boat, Wolf Penniman?" demanded he, leaping down from his high seat the moment he saw me.

"I'm going down to Ruoara on her; that's all I'm doing just now," I replied.

"Did you come to count the passengers?" said he, bitterly.

"I did not, though, for that matter, it would not be a difficult task to count them."

"None of your impudence, Wolf Penniman!"

"What's the matter, Waddie?" I asked, laughing. "I suppose you know I'm not the engineer of the railroad now, and you need not waste any hard words upon me."

"I don't want to see you on this boat, or on our side of the lake," he added, restoring the cigar to his mouth, and looking as magnificent as a little magnate could look.

"I won't hurt you, or the boat."

"I'll bet you won't!"

"This is a splendid boat," I continued, in a conciliatory tone.

"Splendid enough."

"But I don't think you are smart to let the major get ahead of you, as he does."

"What do you mean by that?"

"If I were running this boat, I should have my share of the through passengers," I replied, with all the good-nature I possessed.

"You would do big things!" sneered he.

"I should try to."

"You can't come it over me, as you did over my father."

"I haven't the least desire to come it over you. I expect to go into business on my own account pretty soon," I replied.

"If it hadn't been for me, you would have been captain of this boat," said he, intending to throw his heaviest shot by this remark.

"Well, I suppose you did what you thought was best for the line; and if you are satisfied, I ought to be."

"You didn't make much when you ran away from Centreport."

"Neither did I lose much. If we are both satisfied about that, we need not quarrel."

"I shall always quarrel with you, Wolf Penniman, as long as I live," he added, spitefully. "I hate you!"

"Well, I hope you will have a good time. For my part, I don't hate you, Waddie; and if I had a chance to do you a good turn, I would do it now as quick as ever I would."

"You needn't snuffle to me. I don't ask any favors of you. I am president of the Steamboat Company, and I suppose you would like to have me get down on my knees and beg you to take command of this boat."

"Not much," I replied, laughing.

"You think you are a great man!"

"No, I'm only a boy, like yourself."

"If I had seen you before the boat started, you should not have gone in her."

"That game was tried on the other side of the lake. It don't work well."

"Don't you come on board of this boat again; if you do, we will try it on."

Both of the little magnates down upon me, and I was forbidden to ride in either steamer or cars! Waddie puffed up his cigar and walked away, evidently with the feeling that he was not making much out of me. The Ucayga touched at the wharf, and I went on shore. So did the little magnate of Centreport.

CHAPTER II.

THE AUCTION AT RUOARA.

IT was not yet time for the auction, and I waited on the wharf to see the steamer start. She was still a novelty in Ruoara, and many people came down to the shore to observe her beautiful proportions, and the speed with which she cut through the waters. Hundreds of them made the trip to Ucayga and back for the sole purpose of seeing the boat. After the old steamers were taken off, and before the Ucayga was put on the route, the inhabitants of this town had been obliged to cross the ferry to Grass Springs, and take the trains of the Lake Shore Railroad when they wished to go in either direction. The advent of this palatial steamer was therefore a new era to them, and they regarded her with pride and pleasure.

Ruoara was situated nearly opposite Grass Springs; but the four islands lay off the former town, and a

little below. The South Shoe was due west from the
wharf where the boat touched, and she was obliged to
back, and go over a mile out of her course, to avoid
the island and the shoal water which lay near it. The
South Shoe, therefore, was a nuisance in its relation to
the steamboat navigation of Ruoara. The five minutes which this circuit required had doubtless caused
the Ucayga to miss her connection more than once.

I have been told that I am a machinist by nature.
I do not know how this may be, but I am sure that I
never see a difficulty without attempting to study out
the means to remedy it. As I stood on the wharf,
watching the winding course of the splendid steamer,
I could not help grappling with the problem of saving
this loss of time on the trip. These five minutes
might sometimes enable the boat to win the day in
the competition with the railroad.

As I have hinted before, I knew every foot of bottom in this part of the lake. I had sailed hundreds
of miles among these islands, and, while I was thinking over the matter, the key to the problem flashed
upon my mind. I do not mean to say that it was a
very brilliant idea; but, simple as it was, it had evi-

dently not occurred to the captain of the steamer, who was a Hitaca man, and knew only the ordinary channels of the lake, used by the steamers. I had an idea; but I deemed it wise to keep my own counsel in the matter, for a suggestion from me would probably have been deemed impertinent.

When the Ucayga disappeared behind the South Shoe, I turned my attention to the business which had brought me to Ruoara. A short distance down the lake, and on its bank, was a beautiful and very elaborate cottage, which had evidently been intended as a copy of that occupied by Colonel Wimpleton. Off the lake wall lay the boat which I hoped to purchase. The owner had made an immense "spread," and failed out clean in the height of his glory. People who could afford to purchase such rich and gaudy trappings as those with which the bankrupt owner fitted up his mansion, did not care to buy them at second-hand. Everybody expected that the ornamental appendages of the establishment would be sold for a tithe of their cost; and so they were.

To most of the people on the lake, any boat beyond a skiff for actual service was regarded as a luxury,

especially such a craft as that which floated off the
wall. Taking hold of the painter, I hauled her in, and
stepped on board. She was a very rakish-looking boat,
sloop-rigged, with a cabin forward containing two
berths, and the smallest stove it is possible to imagine.
She was about twenty-four feet long, and as well appointed in every respect as though she had been fitted
up to cross the ocean. The owner had certainly lavished money upon her, which he could afford to do, at
the expense of his creditors.

While I was examining her I saw the crowd of
purchasers moving about the house as the sale proceeded. It was a hopeful sign that no one seemed to
care a straw about the boat. Men and women were
examining everything else about the establishment, but
the Belle — for that was the name I found upon her
stern — was wholly neglected. I continued my examination without the notice of any one for some time.
I took the trap off the well, and got at the bottom. I
found that she was built in the most thorough manner.
I was sure she had cost all of six hundred dollars.

"What are you doing in that boat, Wolf Penniman?"

I raised my head from the diligent search I was making in the bottom of the boat, and discovered Mr. Waddie on the wall.

"I am looking at her," I replied.

"What are you looking at her for?"

"Because I want to see her."

"What do you want to see her for?"

"I take an interest in boats," I answered, not caring to be very communicative with the scion of the Wimpletons.

It immediately occurred to me that Waddie's business at Ruoara was the same as my own, and my heart sank within me, for I could not hope to bid against one who had so much money at his command. But I could not think, for the life of me, why Waddie should want the boat, for he had one of about the same size, which was his own private property. Probably he had taken a fancy to her, as I had.

"Are you going to buy her, Wolf?" asked he, with more interest than he was accustomed to manifest in anything.

"That will depend upon circumstances."

"Who told you that I was going to buy this boat?" demanded he, sharply.

"No one."

"You came up to bid against me!"

"I didn't know you were coming till I saw you here."

"If you bid against me, Wolf Penniman, I'll be the death of you."

"I think not," I replied, laughing at this rash threat.

"I will! You will find me an uglier customer to deal with than you did Tom Toppleton. Do you think I'm going to have you dogging my steps wherever I go."

I could only laugh.

"No one about here wants the boat but me," he added.

"I want her."

"Yes, and you want her only because I do," snarled he.

"It's an open thing, I suppose. This is a public auction; and if you are willing to give more than I can, of course you will have her," I replied.

"If you don't bid against me, she will be knocked off at the first offer."

"We won't quarrel, Waddie."

"Yes, we will, if you bid against me. The auctioneer is coming. You mind what I say. If you bid against me, you will repent it as long as you live."

Such language from an ordinary boy would have been very remarkable; from Waddie it was not at all so. It was his usual style of bullying. It seemed very strange that the young gentleman should attempt to bully me into silence when he could outbid me; but I ascertained afterwards that his father objected to buying the boat, and even refused to furnish the money, so that Waddie could only bid to the extent of the funds then in his possession. However weak and indulgent the colonel was, he had not sunk into the condition of subserviency to his son into which the major had fallen.

The auctioneer, followed by only a small portion of the crowd from the house, approached the spot where Waddie stood. I jumped ashore, and secured a place on the wall. The auctioneer took his stand on the stern of the Belle; but none of the attendants upon the sale felt interest enough to go on board, or even to examine the craft. It was plain enough that the competition lay between Waddie and myself alone. I had made up my mind to lose the boat, and I felt badly about it. I could not expect to bid successfully against the son of the rich man. However, I meant to try, and I only hoped that Waddie would keep his temper. He had certainly given me fair warning; but perhaps it was my misfortune that I did not happen to be afraid of him.

While I stood there, I could not help thinking that I was spoiling all my chances of a situation in the future on board of the Ucayga, if the colonel should again be disposed to repeat his munificent offers. But I had a dream of doing even a better thing with the Belle than I could on board of the steamer or on the Lake Shore Railroad, and without being subject to the caprices of either of the young gentlemen who were so potent in both.

The auctioneer gave us a grandiloquent description of the "fairy pleasure barge" which was before us. He was not a nautical man, and sadly bungled in his terms. She was the fastest sailer on the lake; was a good sea boat. She was right and tight in every respect.

"For, gentlemen," he added, facetiously, "a boat, unlike a man, is a good deal better when she is tight than when she is not tight"— a witticism at which the auctioneer laughed much more heartily than the audi- tors. "She is copper-fastened, besides being fastened to the wall. Like myself, and some of you, gentlemen, she is very sharp. And now, how much am I offered for this magnificent yacht, the finest, without excep- tion, on the lake. What shall I have for her?"

"Twenty-five dollars," said Waddie Wimpleton, who could not conceal his interest and anxiety in the result.

"Did you say twenty-five dollars, Mr. Wimpleton?" said the auctioneer, with a look which was intended to manifest his astonishment at the smallness of the bid. "Why, she cost over six hundred dollars! You can't mean that, Mr. Wimpleton."

"Yes, I do mean it!" said Waddie, smartly.

"Twenty-five dollars is bid for this splendid yacht, sharp as a Yankee pedler, and copper-fastened, besides being fastened to the wall. Who says a hundred?"

No one said a hundred. No one said anything for a few moments, during which time the auctioneer dwelt upon the beautiful proportions of the craft, and repeated his jokes for a third time.

"Only twenty-five dollars is bid for the Belle! Why, gentlemen, that would not pay for one of her sails."

"Thirty dollars," I added.

"Thirty dollars!" repeated the auctioneer, glancing curiously at me. "Perhaps I ought to say that the conditions of this sale are cash on delivery. Thirty dollars! Shall I have a hundred?"

Waddie glanced furiously at me, and I saw that his fists were clinched.

"Thirty-five," said he.

"Forty."

"Forty-five," snapped he.

"Fifty," I added, quietly.

I had hardly uttered the word before Waddie's fist was planted squarely on the end of my nose, and the blood spirted from the member. He was about to follow it up with another, when I deemed it necessary to do something. I parried his stroke, and hit him so fairly in the eye that he reeled, lost his balance, and went over backwards into the lake with a fearful splash.

CHAPTER III.

ON BOARD THE BELLE.

SOMEHOW, when we resort to violence, we often do much more than we intend. I did not desire to do anything more than defend myself; but Waddie stood between me and the water, and when I hit him, he went over. I have never claimed to be saint or angel. I was human enough to "get mad" when the young gentleman flattened my nose, and drew the gore therefrom. I simply defended myself by the only means within my power, though I did not intend to throw Waddie into the lake.

The water was not more than three or four feet deep near the wall; but Waddie might have been drowned in it, if he had not been promptly assisted by the auctioneer and others. But if the water was not deep, it was cold, and hydropathy is an excellent remedy for overheated blood.

"That's the way Wolf fights," said Waddie, as he shook the water from his clothes.

"He served you right," replied the auctioneer, who, I believe, did not belong to Ruoara — certainly not to Centreport.

"Do you call that fair play?" demanded Waddie, with chattering teeth.

"To be sure I do. You turned on him, and hit him without any warning," retorted the auctioneer. "He hit you back, and paid you in your own coin. You went over into the lake, but that was not his fault. Fifty dollars is bid for this beautiful boat, that cost over six hundred."

"I told him I would be the death of him if he bid against me," replied Waddie; but there was not much life in his words.

"O, ho! you did — did you? Well, I'm glad he knocked you into the lake; and if I had known what you told him, you might have staid in the lake for all me," added the auctioneer, indignantly, for the greatest sin in his estimation was a conspiracy to suppress bidding at an auction. "Fifty dollars! Shall I have sixty?"

WHAT HAPPENED AT THE AUCTION. Page 30.

Waddie lingered on the wall, shivering with the cold; but, to my astonishment, he did not make any additional bid. I could not understand it. The auctioneer again called the attention of the audience to the many virtues of the Belle, and then observed, in piteous tones, that only fifty dollars was bid for the beautiful craft.

"I haven't done with you yet, Wolf Penniman," said Waddie, creeping up to me.

"Well, I hope you will finish with me as soon as possible," I replied, stepping back from the wall so as not to afford him any temptation to push me into the lake.

"I'll keep my word with you."

"Fifty dollars!" stormed the auctioneer, justly indignant at the sacrifice of the boat.

"When must it be paid for?" demanded Waddie.

"Cash on delivery," replied the auctioneer, sharply.

"Can it be delivered to-morrow?"

"No; the sale must be closed to-day. Fifty dollars!"

"Sixty," said Waddie, with an ugly glance at me, after one of the bystanders had whispered a word to

3

him, to the effect, I suppose, that he would lend him ten dollars.

"Sixty-five," I added, quietly.

"Sixty-five!" repeated the auctioneer, more hopefully.

Waddie was beginning to warm up again, and had actually ceased to shiver. He spoke to the bystander with whom he was acquainted, and then bid seventy dollars. I immediately advanced to seventy-five.

"Seventy-five!" shouted the auctioneer. "Gentlemen, this is a shameful sacrifice of valuable property."

I saw Waddie's friend shake his head, as though he was not willing to risk more than twenty dollars on the speculation; but while the young gentleman was arguing the point with him, the Belle was struck off to me. The scion of the house of Wimpleton swore like a bad boy when this result was reached. He shook his fist at me, and raised a laugh among the bystanders, not all of whom appeared to reverence the idol which had been set up in Centreport. My purchase included the small boat which served as a tender to the Belle, the mooring buoy, and other appurtenances.

The auctioneer's clerk gave me a bill of sale of the

boat, and I paid the cash on the spot. I was the happiest young man on the shore of the lake. Waddie had disappeared as soon as the sale was completed, and I was subjected to no further annoyance from him. Having finished my business in Ruoara, I was ready to sail for home, and astonish the Middleporters with the sight of my purchase.

"That's a fine boat you have bought," said one of the half dozen persons who stood on the wall watching my movements.

I looked up and saw that the speaker was Dick Bayard, a Wimpletonian, and the senior captain in the Centreport battalion. He was a leading spirit among the students on his side of the lake. He had been the actual, though not the nominal, leader in the war on the Horse Shoe, and had distinguished himself by his energy and enterprise in that memorable conflict. His father lived in Ruoara, which accounted for his appearance there when the Institute was in session. I had a great deal of respect for him, after I saw how well he bore himself in the silly war, though he had always been a strong and unreasonable supporter of Waddie, and had aided him in persecuting me before I was driven out of Centreport.

"Yes, she is a first-rate boat," I replied; for speaking well of my boat was even better than speaking well of my dog.

"Are you going down to Middleport now?"

"Yes; right off."

"Will you take a passenger?" he asked, rather diffidently.

"Who?"

"Myself."

"I will, with pleasure."

"Thank you, Wolf."

I pushed the tender up to the wall, and he stepped into it.

"Some of the fellows say you are not a bit like other boys, Wolf; and I begin to think they are more than half right," said Dick Bayard, as he came on board of the Belle.

"Well, I don't know. I don't suppose I'm very different from other fellows," I replied, with becoming modesty.

"You don't seem to have a grudge against any one. If a fellow abuses you, you treat him as well as ever. You knock him over in self-defence, and then behave towards him just as though nothing had happened."

"I think I can afford to do so."

"I didn't think you would let me sail up the lake with you," laughed he.

"Why not?"

"Like a good many other fellows, I have toadied to Waddie Wimpleton, and helped him hunt you down."

"I don't care anything about that now."

"I see you don't. Can I help you?" he asked, as I began to hoist the mainsail.

"You may take the peak-halyard, if you please."

We hoisted the jib and mainsail, and stood up the lake with a gentle breeze. I took the elaborately carved tiller in my hand, and if ever a young man was proud of his boat, his name was Wolfert Penniman. The Belle fully realized all even of the auctioneer's enthusiastic description.

"Don't you belong to the Institute now, Dick?" I asked, after we had said all that it was necessary to say in praise of the Belle, and after my companion had related to me more of her history than I knew before.

"Not much," said he, laughing; "my name is still on the books, and I am still captain of Company A, Wimpleton Battalion; but I don't go to school half the time."

"Why not?" I asked, curiously.

"I don't want to. Since the Steamboat Company was formed, Waddie has put on so many airs that some of us can't stand it. In fact, our president does not treat us much better than he did you."

"That is unfortunate for you, and still more so for him."

"They say the Toppletonians are down upon Tommy; but I am inclined to think the feeling is worse on our side than on yours. Waddie is the most unpopular fellow on our side of the lake."

"I have often wondered how you fellows, whose fathers are rich men, could let Waddie lord it over you as he does. My father is a poor man, but I can't stand it."

"They won't stand it much longer," replied Dick, shaking his head. "Our fellows have had about enough of it."

"What are you going to do?" I inquired.

"Well, I don't exactly know, and if I did, I suppose it would not be prudent to tell you," laughed Dick. "They are going to turn him out of office, for one thing."

" I think that would do him good.   That same thing will happen to Tommy Toppleton at the next election."

" Waddie got into a row the other day with a lot of fellows that don't belong to the Institute.   He under-took to drive them off the ground where they were playing, near the town school.   They wouldn't go, and one of them, a plucky little fellow, spoke his mind pretty freely to him.   Waddie and one of his cronies caught him the next day, and gave him a cowhiding. The town fellows mean to pay him off, and I know they will."

" They will only get into trouble.   Waddie's father will stand by him," I added.

" I don't know what they mean to do."

" What did Waddie want to drive the town fellows off the ground for ? " I inquired.

" They were playing ball, and Waddie wanted the ground to have a game with his friends."

" Whose ground was it ? "

" It was the piece of land called the school pasture, and belongs to the town.   You know where it is."

" I know the place."

" One party had just as good a right to the ground

as the other; but you know how Waddie does things.
If he wants anything, he takes it, and makes a row if
everybody don't yield to him."

"That's his style."

"But don't say anything about what I've said,
please. If anything happens to Waddie, it will be
laid to these fellows."

"They ought to have been smart enough to keep
still themselves," I replied.

"One of them told me about it in confidence. I
shouldn't have said anything to you, if you lived on
our side now."

"I won't say anything."

I was not likely to think anything more about it,
and still less to meddle with the affair.

"We are tired of this thing on our side of the lake,"
continued Dick. "If we had twenty fellows that
would serve Waddie as you did to-day, when he
pitched into you, we might make a decent fellow of
him after a while. For my own part, I don't mean to
take a word of lip from him. If he insults me, I shall
give him as good as he sends. Indeed, I have done so
once or twice, and he hates me like poison for it."

" I don't think you make anything by using hard words."

" What do you do, Wolf? "

" I don't think that abusive language does me any harm, and I mean to be good-natured, whatever happens; though, when it comes to hitting me in the face, and giving me a bloody nose, I can't quite stand that, and I defend myself as vigorously as I know how. I think a fellow can be a gentleman without putting his neck under anybody's heel."

I landed Dick Bayard at Centreport, and stood over to the other side of the lake. I moored the Belle in a little bay not far from my father's house, and went home to report my good fortune.

CHAPTER IV.

THE SCENE IN THE PICNIC GROVE.

O F course I thought of but little except my boat after she came into my possession, and before the day closed I had exhibited her to all who felt an interest in such matters. My father was delighted with her, and congratulated me on the bargain I had made. Tom Walton declared that the Belle was the finest craft on the lake. Before night, so thoroughly had my boat been talked up in Middleport, I had a party engaged for the next day, to visit the fishing-grounds.

After seeing the boat, and discussing the matter with my father, I had the conscience to fix the price of her at seven dollars a day, which included my own services. When a gentleman spoke of engaging her for a week or more, I told him he should have her for five dollars a day for any longer period than three days.

The weather was very warm and pleasant for October, and my first trip to the fishing-grounds was a great success. My party were delighted with the boat, and I did all I could to make them comfortable. The gentlemen had a good time, and spoke so favorably of the Belle and of me, that the person who proposed to go for a week closed the bargain with me, and I was engaged to start on Monday morning. I was in a fair way to get back, before the season closed, what I had paid for the boat.

On Saturday I had no engagement; but I found it quite impossible to keep out of the Belle. I intended to go on an exploring expedition up the lake, in order to find some good landing-places. I went after Tom Walton, to give him an invitation to accompany me; but I found he was at work for a day or two in one of the stores. The wind blew quite fresh from the northwest, and the lake was tolerably rough, which made me the more desirous of testing the qualities of the Belle.

While I was reefing down the mainsail, I saw the Highflyer pass the Narrows, headed up the lake. This was Waddie Wimpleton's boat. She was about the

size of the Belle, and I could not see why the young
gentleman wanted the latter. The Highflyer would
certainly have satisfied me, though in the course of the
day I was better informed in regard to his motives.
Waddie had reefed his mainsail, and was going at a
rapid rate up the lake.

I had no wish to come into collision with him,
though I was rather anxious to know which boat could
make the best time. He was alone; indeed, I had
often noticed that he sailed without any company;
and, as neither of the Institutes was in session on
Saturdays, I had often seen him bound up the lake on
that day. He had the reputation of being a good
boatman, and certainly he had had experience enough
to qualify him to act in that capacity.

I cast off the moorings of the Belle, and stood out
into the lake, where I could get the full benefit of the
wind. Waddie was some distance ahead of me; but
I soon saw that his eye was upon me. I intended to
keep well over on the west side of the lake, so as to
avoid him. I needed not the express declaration he
had made to assure me that he hated me, and that he
would use all possible means to annoy and punish me.

Although I was not afraid of him, I did not wish to afford him any opportunity to gratify his malignity upon me.

He sailed the Highflyer very well. Every minute he glanced at the Belle, to ascertain what progress she was making. Probably he supposed that I had put off for the sole purpose of racing with him, which, however, was not true, though I was very glad of a chance to measure paces with him. Neither of us was obliged to wait long for a decided result, for in half an hour from the time I started, the two boats were abreast of each other, though still half a mile apart. Then the reason why he wished to purchase the Belle was apparent. She was faster than the Highflyer; and Waddie did not enjoy being beaten by any boat on the lake.

Though I was not near enough to observe the effect upon him, I had no doubt he was foaming and fuming with wrath at the audacity of a poor boy like me, who ventured to beat him. While I was walking by him with perfect ease, he threw his boat up into the wind, and turned out the reef in the mainsail. The wind was freshening every hour, and I regarded this as a very

imprudent step on his part. In fact, I began to feel
that I might, in some way, be held responsible for any
disaster which should happen to him, if by racing with
him I goaded him on to any rashness. I therefore
came about, and began to beat down the lake, to assure him that I was not inclined to race under whole
sail in such a blow.

When he had shaken out his reef, however, he gave
chase to me. The Highflyer labored heavily in the
rough waves, and I was not sure that the duty of
rescuing her rash skipper from a watery grave would
not soon devolve upon me. He followed, and having
all sail on his boat, he gained upon me on the wind.
At this rate he would soon be crowing over me, and
the reputation of the Belle would be injured. I was
averse to being beaten, even under a reefed mainsail.
I let out my sheet, and stood over towards the eastern
shore. Waddie followed me, and as I could not now
decline the race on his terms, I soon headed the Belle
up the lake.

By the time I had laid my course, the Highflyer was
abreast of me. Now both of us had the wind on the
quarter. A boat on the wind, with all sail set, can be

better handled than when going before it. I saw the
Highflyer plunging down deep into the waves; but I
suppose Waddie had not learned that a boat over-
pressed in a blow does not make any better time than
one carrying just sail enough to make her go comfortably, without wasting her headway in dives and
plunges. On this tack he no longer gained upon me.
On the contrary, it was soon evident that the Belle
was running away from him. My boat was good for
at least one more mile in five than the Highflyer.

I ran away from Waddie, and went up the lake as
far as Gulfport. I soon lost sight of him, and I concluded that he had made a landing somewhere on the
shore. It was too rough to explore the coast, for the
wind was driving the waves upon the rocks and
beaches with savage power, and it was not prudent
to go too near the land. I put the Belle about, and
commenced beating down the lake. I thought no
more of Waddie, my mind being wholly taken up in
sailing my boat, and in the pleasant anticipation of
making a profitable thing of her.

On the eastern shore of the lake, between Centreport and Gulfport, there was a wood, covering, per-

haps, a square mile of land.   It was much used by picnic parties in the summer, and had a cook-house for
frying fish and making chowders.   A rude landing-
place had been prepared for steamers, for the deep
water extended quite up to the shore.   In the process
of beating the Belle down the lake, I ran her close up
to the pier off the grove.   As I was coming about, I
heard a cry which seemed to indicate great distress.
I was startled by the sound; but, as there were neither
Indians nor wild beasts in the vicinity, I concluded
that I had mistaken the nature of the call.

I was proceeding on my course when the cry was
repeated.   It was certainly the sound of mingled anger
and distress.   I threw the Belle up into the wind, and
listened.   The cry was repeated, and I stood in towards the shore.   Passing the pier, I saw Waddie's
boat secured to the logs.   Just above the wharf there
was a little land-locked bay, into which I ran the Belle.
The cry of distress was not again repeated; but my
curiosity was fully aroused.   I concluded that Waddie
had found some boy or girl, smaller and weaker than
himself, and was exercising the evil propensities of his
nature upon his victim.

I lowered my sails, and secured them. Fastening the painter of the Belle to a tree, I walked towards the cook-house, with the small boat-hook, not bigger than a broom-handle, in my hand. I must say that I dreaded a conflict of any description with Mr. Waddie. There was no more reason in him than in a stone wall, and he really delighted in torturing a victim. If any one interfered to repress his cruelty, he took the act as a personal insult, and regarded himself as oppressed by not being allowed to exercise his malice upon the weak.

I walked cautiously towards the spot from which the cry had come, for I wished to obtain a view of the situation before I was seen myself. The trees were large, and afforded me abundant concealment. Every few moments I stopped to listen; and I soon heard several voices, some of them peculiarly gruff and unnatural. It was plain that Waddie and his victim were not the only actors in the scene. Placing myself behind a tree, I took a careful observation, and discovered smoke rising among the branches; but I could not yet see who the speakers were. Something was

4

going on ; but whether it was a comedy or a tragedy
I could not determine.

I continued cautiously to approach the spot, and
soon gained a position where I could obtain a full view
of the scene. I had expected to find Waddie persecuting some poor wretch. The "boot was on the
other leg." The scion of the house of Wimpleton was
the victim, and not the oppressor. The world seemed
to be turned upside down. Waddie, divested of all
his clothing but his shirt and pants, was tied to a tree.
Near him a fire was snapping and crackling, while over
it hung a kettle. Although I was at the windward of
the fire, the odor which pervaded the woods assured
me that the kettle was filled with tar.

Around the fire were four stout boys, rigged out in
fantastic garments, their faces covered with masks and
other devices to conceal their identity. Near the fire
lay a couple of bolsters, which, no doubt, were filled
with feathers. One of these fellows was stirring the
contents of the kettle, and another was replenishing
the fire, while the other two looked on. Who they
were I could form no idea, for their strange uniforms
completely disguised them.

Waddie looked like the very picture of hopeless misery. I had never seen such an aspect of utter despair on his face. He was as pale as death, and I could even see the tremors of his frame as he trembled with terror.

CHAPTER V.

THE BATTLE WITH WORDS.

I WAS not quite willing to believe that the four stout fellows in the vicinity of the kettle really intended to " tar and feather " Waddie Wimpleton. In the first place, it was astounding that any one on the Centreport side of the lake should have the audacity to conceive such an outrage upon the sacred person of the magnate's only son. Why, the people generally held the great man in about the same reverence as the people of England hold their queen. The idea of committing any indignity upon his person, or upon the persons of any of his family, seemed too mon-strous to be entertained.

I judged that the scene before me was the sequel to the incident of which Dick Bayard had told me. But the actors were Centreporters, and it was amazing to think that even four boys in the whole town could actually undertake to revenge themselves upon Mr. Waddie. All that I had done in my quarrel with him was in self-defence, and the scene transpiring before me was quite incomprehensible.

Perhaps what Dick Bayard had told me in some measure explained the situation. It was a fact that the students of the Wimpleton Institute were in a state of rebellion so far as Waddie was concerned, and the influence of this spirit had doubtless extended beyond the borders of the academy. If the Wimpletonians were audacious enough to think of mutiny against the young lordling, it was not strange that others, not immediately associated with him, should even outdo their own intentions.

The particular school where Waddie had driven the boys from their ball grounds was near the outskirts of the village, and was attended by the sons of some of the farmers living far enough from the centre of influence to be in a measure beyond its sphere. After all, perhaps it is really more singular that any American boys could be found who would submit to the tyranny and domineering of Waddie, than that a few should be found who were willing to resist it to the last extremity.

Strange as the phenomenon seemed to be to one who for years had witnessed the homage paid to Waddie Wimpleton and Tommy Toppleton, the fact was undeniable. The little magnate of Centreport was there, bound fast to a tree. The young ruffians, who were so intent upon retaliating for the injury inflicted upon them, had probably lain in wait at this unfrequented place, perhaps for several weeks. I had heard the screams of their victim when they captured him, and I was sure that he had not yielded without a rugged resistance.

The fire blazed under the tar-kettle, and the preparations were rapidly progressing. I kept in my covert, and watched with breathless interest the proceedings. So completely were the actors disguised that I could not recognize a single one of them. So far as Waddie was concerned, I could not be supposed to have any deep interest in his fate. Perhaps the humiliating and disgusting operation which the ruffians intended to perform would do him good.

I ought to say here that the newspapers, at about this time, were filled with the details of such an indignity inflicted upon an obnoxious person in another part of the Union. Probably some of these boys had read the account, and it had suggested to them a suitable punishment for Waddie. I had seen the narrative myself, but only with contempt for the persecutors, and sympathy for their victim.

Certainly these boys had no right to inflict such an outrage upon Waddie. Though he had been no friend of mine, and though, on the contrary, he gloried in being my enemy, I pitied him. If I did anything for him, it would be just like him to kick me the next day for my pains. I had stumbled upon the scene by accident, but it seemed to me that I had a duty to perform — a duty from which my unpleasant relations with the victim did not absolve me.

Should I interfere to prevent this indignity? My mother was not present, but it seemed to me that I could hear her voice saying to me, in the gentlest of human tones, "Love your enemies." I saw her before me, reading from the New Testament the divine message. Then she seemed to look up from the book, and say to me, "Wolfert, if Christ could forgive and bless even those who sought to slay Him, can you not lift one of your fingers to help one who has wronged you?"

The duty seemed to be very plain, though I could not help thinking that Waddie would insult me the next moment after I had served him, just as Tommy Toppleton had done when I rescued him from his captors on the lake. No matter! I must do my duty, whether he did his or not. I was responsible for my own actions, not for his.

This conclusion was happily reached; but then it was not so easy to act upon its behests. Four stout fellows were before me, either of whom was a full match for me. What could I do against the whole of them? Perhaps nothing; perhaps I could not save Waddie from his fate; but it was none the less my duty to try, even at the expense of some hard knocks. I had the little boat-hook in my hand. It was an insignificant weapon with which to fight four times my own force. But somehow I felt that I was in the right; I felt the inspiration of a desire to do a good deed, and I had a vague assurance that help would in some manner come to me, though from what direction I could not imagine, for at this season of the year few people ever visited the picnic grove.

Leaving the shadow of the tree, which had concealed me from the young ruffians, I walked boldly towards them. The tramp of my feet on the crackling sticks instantly attracted their attention. To my great satisfaction they suddenly retreated into a little thicket near the tar-kettle.

"Save me, Wolf! Save me!" cried Waddie, in tones of the most abject despondency. "Save me, and I will be your best friend."

I did not believe in any promises he could make; but I directed my steps towards him, with the intention of releasing him.

"Stop!" shouted one of the ruffians, in a singularly gruff voice, which afforded me no clew to the owner's identity.

I halted and looked towards the thicket.

"It's only Wolf Penniman," said one of the party, who spoke behind the mask that covered his face. "It's all right. He'll help us do it."

"What are you going to do?" I demanded, pretty sharply.

"We are only paying off Waddie. Will you help us, Wolf?" replied one of the conspirators.

"No, certainly not. You have no right to meddle with him."

"Well, we are going to do it, whether we have any right or not. We will tar and feather him, as sure as he lives."

"Who are you?" I asked, innocently.

"No matter who we are. Has Waddie any right to insult us? Has he any right to cowhide a fellow smaller than he is, within an inch of his life?"

"No; but two wrongs don't make a right, any how you can fix it. Don't you think it is mean for four great fellows like you to set upon one, and abuse him?" I asked.

"It isn't any meaner than what Waddie did, any how. We mean to teach him that he can't trample upon us fellows, and drive us around like slaves. We have stood this thing long enough, and we mean to show him that the knife cuts both ways," replied the fellow with the gruffest voice.

"I don't see it. I haven't any doubt Waddie has imposed upon you; but I think he has used me as badly as he ever did any other fellow. I don't believe in this sort of thing."

"I never will do it again, Wolf, if you will save me this time," pleaded poor Waddie, in piteous tones.

" Well, it's none of your business, Wolf Penniman, and you can leave," added the speaker.

"I think you had better let Waddie go this time. I'll go bail for him, if you will," I continued, good-naturedly, for I was not disposed to provoke a conflict with the ruffians.

"Not if we know it! We have watched too long to catch him to let him go now," replied the gruff-toned ruffian, emerging from the bushes, followed by his companions.

They halted between Waddie and me, and I tried to make out who they were; but they were so effectually disguised that all my scrutiny was baffled. I have since come to the conclusion that I had never been acquainted with them, and so far as I know, no one ever found out who they were. I resorted to the most persuasive rhetoric in my power to induce the ruffians to forego their barbarous purpose; but they were obdurate and inflexible. I tried to give them a Sunday school lesson, and they laughed at me. I endeavored to point out to them the consequences of the act, assuring them that Colonel Wimpleton would leave no measure untried to discover and punish them.

"We'll risk all that," replied the leading ruffian, impatiently. "Now, dry up, Wolf Penniman. We don't wish any harm to you; but you shall not spoil this game. Come, fellows, bring up the tar-kettle."

The wretch went up to Waddie, whose hands were tied behind him, and began to pull off his shirt. The unhappy victim uttered the most piercing screams, and struggled like a madman to break away from the tree.

"This thing has gone far enough," I interposed, indignantly, as a couple of the rascals took the tar-kettle from the fire, and began to carry it towards the tree.

"What are you going to do about it?" blustered the chief of the party.

"I am going to stop it," I replied, smartly.

"I guess not! If you don't take yourself off, we'll give you a coat of the same color."

I rushed up to the two boys who were carrying the kettle, and began to demonstrate pretty freely with the boat-hook. They placed their burden on the ground, and stood by to defend it. I hooked into it with my weapon, and upset it.

CHAPTER VI.

THE BATTLE WITH BLOWS.

THE gruff-voiced conspirator rushed furiously towards me, and I retreated a few paces. The two in charge of the tar-kettle picked it up, and saved a portion of its contents. My heavy assailant was roused to a high pitch of anger by the opposition I made to his plans, and seemed to be disposed to proceed to extremities. He had picked up a club, and continued to advance. Once or twice he made a pass at me with his weapon, but I dodged the blow.

I was not angry, and I was cool. I saw that my foe was clumsy, if he was stout. As he threw his heavy cowhide boots about, he reminded me of an elephant dancing a hornpipe. I saw two or three chances to hit him, but I refrained from doing so, for I did not want a broken head upon my conscience.

"Come here, Martin!" shouted he to one of

his fellow-conspirators; and this was the only name I heard used during the whole of the strife.

"Why don't you knock him?" demanded the person called, as he sprang forward to assist the big fellow.

I continued to retreat, and intended to fall back upon my boat for protection; but the second assailant got in behind me, and presently I saw more stars than I was anxious to behold in broad daylight. I concluded that I was a fool to indulge in squeamishness on such an occasion, when my head was in danger of being "caved in" by the heavy blows of the rascals. Besides, the rap I had received on the sconce had a tendency to rouse my ire; in fact, it did rouse it; and at the next convenient opportunity, I struck the big fellow a smart blow on the head. Evidently it hit him in a tender place, for he dropped flat upon the ground.

I was alarmed at this catastrophe, and fortunately the second assailant was affected in the same way. I had secured a position where I could not be attacked in the rear, and having disposed of the heaviest of my foes, I turned upon the other. The fate of his companion was a salutary lesson to him, and he retired to the side of the fallen champion.

But the big fellow was not so badly damaged as I had feared. He was not even stunned, and soon sprang to his feet, rubbing his head, and endeavoring to collect his scattered ideas. My own head felt as though a cannon ball had dropped upon it. I took off my cap and examined the place with my hand. There was a big "bump" on the side of my head to certify the damage I had received.

"Come up here, fellows!" shouted the leader in the enterprise, with a savage oath, when he had in some measure recovered from the shock of the blow I had given him.

They arranged their disguises anew, and held a consultation. I could not hear what they said, but I knew that I was the subject of their remarks. Each of them then provided himself with a club, and I realized that they intended to make an organized attack upon me. If they captured me, my chances of being tarred and feathered were about as good as those of Waddie. It would have been the most prudent thing I could do to retire from the field, and permit the party to carry out their vicious purpose upon the little magnate of Centreport. Though I had been "punished" as much as I cared for, I felt so much interest in the affair that I was not willing to leave.

I saw two of the party, who had not before been engaged, start at a smart run, with the evident intention of getting between me and the water. I broke into a run myself, and made for the boat. Jumping on board, I pushed her off far enough to save me from molestation. But then I observed that the other two ruffians had not engaged in the pursuit. The two who had done so stationed themselves on the bank of the lake, and appeared to be so well satisfied that I began to think something was wrong.

Suddenly it flashed upon my mind that the big fellow intended to outwit me; that he and his companion would do the dirty job while my two guards kept me at a safe distance. Having put my hand to the plough, I had too much pride, if not principle, to permit myself to be outflanked in this manner. As the case now stood, the big ruffian had won the battle. I was disgusted with myself, and hastened to retrieve the mistake I had made. I pushed the boat in towards the shore, and my two sentinels stepped down to meet me.

"That's a fine boat you have, Wolf," said one of them, good-naturedly, as he leaped on the half-deck.

The other one followed him, and I deemed it wise to pick up my boat-hook.

"She is fine enough," I replied.

"Will you let us look at her?" said the speaker, winking at the other.

What did he wink for? That was what I wanted to know. Why were they so good-natured? It was not a very difficult problem, after all. Why should they not be good-natured, if they could keep me where I was while their companions did their vile work upon Waddie? They were smart — they were!

"Certainly you may look at her, if you like," I replied, very pleasantly, all of a sudden, for I intended to be as smart as I could.

"They say you are a first-rate fellow, Wolf," continued the one who had first stepped on board, as he jumped down into the standing-room, where I was.

5

"O, I am!"

"I can't see why you stick up for such a mean shote as Waddie Wimpleton."

"I don't stick up for him. I only like to see a fellow have fair play," I replied, seating myself, as though I had nothing more to desire or hope for.

"He don't give anybody fair play. This is about the best boat I ever saw," the speaker added, as he looked into the little cabin.

"She is first rate," I answered, carelessly.

"Cabin, beds, carpet, stove."

"Yes, and there is a chance to set a table there," I went on, after the second guard had contrived to push the boat away from the shore, as he supposed without attracting my attention. "Go in, if you like, and I will show you how we dine on board of the Belle."

I spoke with becoming enthusiasm about the boat and her fixtures, and I think my guests believed that they had drawn away my attention from Waddie. At any rate, the first speaker went into the cabin, and, at my suggestion, the second one followed him.

"Now, do you see that board, which is turned up against the mast?" I proceeded, as I pointed to the table.

Yes, I see it."

"Well, just turn the button and let it down."

It stuck pretty tight, as I knew it would, and both of them took hold to lower the board. While they were thus engaged, I drew the slide, and banged the doors to, before they suspected what I was doing. Slipping in the padlock, I locked it, and while my guards were turning the table in the cabin, I performed the same office outside. They were prisoners, and I felt that I might reasonably expect to find them where I had left them. They might damage the cabin of the Belle, but that was all they could do.

I hauled the boat in, and, as I leaped on shore, I heard another piercing scream from Waddie, which assured me that the tragedy had been renewed. I leaped on the land, and, with the boat-hook still in my hand, hastened to the scene of active operations. As I approached the spot, I saw the two ruffians tearing Waddie's clothes from his back, in readiness to apply the tar-swab. The wretched victim screamed piteously. I saw that I had no time to trifle with the affair. I decided to be the aggressor this time. I rushed furiously at the big fellow whom I had hit before. He did not see me till I was within fifty feet of him. He had laid aside his club, and I " pitched in." I dealt him a heavy blow on the side of his head, and he retreated to the place where he had left his weapon. I made at the other one then; but the terrors of the boat-hook were too much for him, and he fled to obtain his club.

While they were falling back upon their ammunition, I took my knife from my pocket, and, rushing up to the tree, cut the cord which confined Waddie. He was free; but his hands were still tied together. I . told him to follow me; and, gaining a moment's time, I released his hands.

" I'll never forget this, Wolf," said he. " I will not, as true as I live."

" We haven't got out of the scrape yet. Pick up that stick, and keep close to me. We must fight it out now."

" I'll fight as long as I can stand," he replied, resolutely.

The fellow with the gruff voice swore like a pirate when he saw that Waddie was free, and he and his companion immediately gave chase to us. I had no longer any reason to fight, and I was not disposed to do so, except in self-defence; but I was determined to bring off Waddie unharmed, whatever happened.

We made a detour towards my boat, closely pursued by the two ruffians, now foaming with rage at the failure of their wicked scheme. We outran them, and soon had placed a sufficient distance between us and them to justify a halt. But we were not a great way from the boat.

"What has become of the other two fellows?" asked Waddie, puffing under the exhaustion of his hard run.

"They are safe," I replied; and involuntarily I put my hand into my pocket to search for the key of the padlock on the cabin slide.

"Where are they?"

"In my boat, locked up in the cabin."

I continued to fumble in my pockets for the key; but I could not find it, and the conclusion was forced upon me that I had stupidly left it in the lock. If my two guards could not release themselves, this service could easily be performed by their associates. I had made a bad mistake; though, after all, the blunder would only save them the trouble of breaking the lock, and otherwise damaging the boat.

I found that keeping still was the best method of baffling our pursuers, since they had evidently lost sight of us. I heard their voices, but the sound receded, and it was plain that they were moving towards the lake.

CHAPTER VII.

WADDIE AND I.

AS nearly as I could judge in our place of concealment, the big fellow, who was the leading spirit of the conspirators, had been careful to keep the inside line of retreat from the tar-kettle to the boat. Of course he expected us to retire in that direction; but when we distanced him in the chase, he had moved directly to the water side, while I had swept around in a much larger circle. As soon as he lost sight of us in the thick undergrowth, which had only been cut away on a few acres composing the picnic grounds, he had made the shortest line for the boats.

"Where is your boat, Wolf?" asked Waddie, who was actually trembling with apprehension, though I could not blame him for being alarmed, since the villains were still on his track, and still intent upon subjecting him to the degrading ordeal.

"It lies about a quarter of a mile below yours, at the wharf," I replied to my trembling companion.

"What shall we do?"

"We must keep still for a little while, till we see a good chance to reach the boat."

"I am cold, Wolf," said he.

Perhaps he offered this as an explanation of his shaking condition; but, although the weather was pleasant for the season, it was still chilly enough to render thick clothing quite comfortable. Above his boots the poor fellow had on nothing but his shirt and pants, and the former had been torn half off by the wretches who persecuted him. I took off the heavy sack I wore, and gave it to him.

"You will be cold yourself, Wolf," said he, with a degree of consideration of which I did not believe him capable.

"No; I can get along very well. Put it on."

"Thank you, Wolf; you are very kind."

Those were amazing words to be uttered by him to me! But his father had been even more gentle, and had apparently forgotten all about me in a few days. He put on my coat, which fitted him very well, and I buttoned it up to the throat for him. He declared that it "felt good;" and I have no doubt it did, for the driving wind upon his bare shoulders must have been anything but comfortable.

"Do you know any of those fellows?" asked Waddie.

"I do not. I heard the big fellow call one of the others Martin, but I haven't the least idea who any of them are. I suppose they belong on your side of the lake, and I haven't seen much of the fellows there lately," I replied.

"Do you think they belong to our Institute?"

"I don't believe they do. They are coarser, rougher fellows than the students on either side."

"I should like to know who they are," added Waddie, compressing his lips and shaking his head. "But whoever they are, if they don't have to suffer for this, you may set me down for a ninny."

"I think we had better get out of the scrape before we·say much about punishing them. I am inclined to believe that big fellow will suffer from a sore head for a few weeks to come. I cracked him hard with this boat-hook."

"Perhaps this sore head will enable us to find out who he is."

"I hope so; but these fellows have been pretty cunning. I heard one of them say they had been on the watch for you several weeks."

"I was a fool to come ashore here."

"I don't know why you were, unless you suspected something of this kind."

"I hadn't the remotest suspicion of anything. I don't know of any reason why they should wish to treat me in this manner. I haven't done anything to them."

"But you don't know who they are."

"Well, I haven't done anything to any fellows."

"Are you sure of that, Waddie?"

"I don't remember anything."

"You don't?" And it seemed very strange to me that he had forgotten the facts related to me by Dick Bayard.

"No, I don't. Do you think I would lie about it?" retorted he, in a tone and manner which seemed quite natural to me.

"Didn't you and some one else cowhide one of the town fellows some time ago?"

"O, that was four or five weeks ago. It couldn't have anything to do with that."

"Perhaps it may. These fellows say they have been on the lookout for you for weeks."

"I had forgotten about that," said he, looking meditative, and, I thought, chagrined. "But those fellows insulted me, especially a young cub, who threatened to thrash me. I gave him a dose the next day, which I think he will remember when he wants to be impudent to me."

"Precisely so! And I am only surprised that you did not remember it yourself, when you were tied to that tree with the tar-kettle before you."

"Do you really believe that fellow is at the bottom of this affair?" asked Waddie, knitting his brows.

"I don't know anything about it."

"But that fellow was smaller than any of these."

"Of course I can give you no information, for I don't know any of them. But we will talk over that matter another time. You stay where you are, Waddie, and I will take an observation."

I crept for some distance through the cowpath in the underbrush, till I heard voices near the lake. I

could not see the ruffians, but I judged by the sound
that they were moving towards the wharf where
Waddie's boat was moored. I proceeded still far
ther towards the lake, and, emerging from the bushes,
I discovered all four of the wretches on the wharf.
The two whom I had imprisoned in the cabin of the
Belle had broken out, as I had anticipated, or possibly
the other two had released them. I feared that they
had ruined or badly damaged my boat, and I was very
anxious about her.

I hastened back to the spot where I had left Waddie, and conducted him to a position near the open
woods. I did not think it expedient to exhibit ourselves yet, and we waited an hour or more in our concealment. I could not see Waddie's persecutors.
They did not attempt any further pursuit. Probably
they supposed we had started on foot for Centreport,
and doubtless they deemed it proper to consider what
steps were necessary to insure their own safety, for
they knew very well that Colonel Wimpleton would
turn out the whole town in pursuit of them as soon as
he heard of the attempted outrage.

"By the great horn spoon," exclaimed Waddie,

who was becoming very impatient after an hour's anxious waiting, " there they are, going off in my boat ! "

" Good ! " I replied. " They couldn't do anything that would suit me better; that is, if they have not sunk or smashed the Belle."

This thought gave me a severe pang, and I almost groaned as I thought of my beautiful craft ruined by these malignant wretches.

" No matter if they have, Wolf. My father will pay for making her as good as ever she was," said Waddie.

" But I am engaged to go up the lake in her with a party on Monday morning."

" We will pay all damages, so that you shall not lose a penny. But I'll bet you won't want to go up the lake next week in the Belle," he added, warmly.

I did not care to follow up the significance of this remark, for I had not much confidence in the fair-weather promises of the Wimpletons. I judged that he intended to do some great thing for me. Perhaps he only flattered himself that he meant to be magnanimous and generous. He was as impulsive in his loves as in his hates; and, though he adhered to the latter with extraordinary tenacity, the former cooled off very suddenly.

"Do you suppose those fellows know how to handle a boat?" I continued, as I saw Waddie's sloop go out into the lake under full sail.

"I hope not," replied he, with energy. "But I wish they were in your boat, instead of mine, for then they would go to the bottom if they upset her."

"I hope they won't be drowned," I added, as the boat heeled over so that her gunwale went under.

"I don't care if they are."

"Be reasonable, Waddie."

"I am reasonable. What do you suppose I care for the villains, after what they have done to me?"

"Love your enemies, Waddie. Return good for evil."

"It's easy enough to talk; but I don't believe much in that sort of stuff."

"It isn't stuff, Waddie. If I had acted on your principle, you would have been tarred and feathered before this time."

"You won't lose anything by what you have done, Wolf," replied he, rather sheepishly.

"I don't expect to make anything by it."

"You will."

"That isn't the idea. If I had acted on your plan, I should have taken hold and helped those fellows impose upon you. I don't ask or expect anything for what I have done. I have made enemies of these chaps, whoever they are, for the sake of one who drove me out of Centreport, hit me a crack in the face the other day, and tells me squarely that he hates me."

"You wait, Wolf, and see what you will see."

"I don't ask anything, and I won't take anything for what I have done. I only want you to have ideas a little different about other people."

"It's no use of talking; you may be a saint, but I can't be one," said Waddie, impatiently. "I think those fellows will swamp the boat; but she has air-tanks, and can't sink."

"We needn't stay here any longer. You can go up town in my boat. I think we may as well be ready to pick those fellows up when they upset."

"I will try to find my clothes," said Waddie, as he moved off towards the tar-kettle.

I went down to my boat. She lay just as I had left her, except that the two glass ports in the trunk of the cabin were broken. The prisoners had evidently attempted to reach the lock by thrusting their arms through these apertures. Whether they succeeded or not, or whether they were released by their companions outside, I do not know. Beyond the breaking of the glass no injury had been done to the Belle. The padlock and key were both there. I hoisted my reefed mainsail, and stood up to the wharf, towards which Waddie was now walking, with his coat and vest on his arm.

CHAPTER VIII.

THE WRECK OF THE HIGHFLYER.

WHEN I ran the Belle out of the little inlet in which I had moored her, I found that the wind had been increasing, and the waves were really quite savage. My first solicitude was in regard to the ruffians in Waddie's boat; for, whatever they deserved in the way of punishment, it was terrible to think of their being ingulfed in the raging waters. I soon obtained a view of them. They had lowered the sail, and were tossing madly about on the waves. Of course the craft was no longer under control, if it had been since the rogues embarked in her, and she appeared to be drifting rapidly towards the land.

The line of the shore in this part of the lake extended about north-west and south-east. Without knowing anything at all about a boat, the conspirators against the peace and dignity of Waddie Wim-

6

pletion had run out from the wharf, keeping the wind on the beam. Doubtless the furious movements of the boat astonished them. It must have shaken them up to a degree they had never before experienced; but they were reckless fellows, and perhaps believed that this was the ordinary behavior of a boat when the breeze was fresh.

They were not far from right in this respect; but they ought to have known that a boat needs skilful handling at such a time. They had continued on their course about half way across the lake. They did not seem to know enough to ease off the sheet when the heavy flaws came, or to "touch her up" with the helm. When it came so heavy that they could stand it no longer, they lowered the sail. A boat without any sail on, even in a blow, is as bad as an unruly horse without a bridle. She must have steerage-way, or she cannot be controlled. She was now in the trough of the sea, rolling helplessly in the billows — now dipping in the water on one side, and now on the other.

When I ran in at the pier, Waddie jumped on board of the Belle. He had put on his coat and vest, but still complained that he was very cold. I had some old coats in my cabin, which I offered to him, and, though they were not fashionable garments, he was glad to avail himself of my wardrobe.

"It blows heavier than ever, Waddie," I said, while he was putting on one of the ragged and weather-stained overcoats.

"If you can't run up to town, I can go on shore and walk up," he replied, glancing at the angry lake.

"O, I can go it well enough; but I was thinking of those fellows out there."

"I shall not waste much fine feeling upon them, you had better believe!"

"They have lowered the sail, and are rolling about there like mud turtles on a log. The boat must be full of water."

"She will not sink, and as long as they hold on they will be safe enough."

"I am not so sure of that, Waddie. They are drifting like mad towards the rocky point above Gulf-port. If they run your boat on those sharp rocks, it will be all day with them."

"I don't care for the boat."

"You don't want her smashed — do you?"

"I don't care if she is. She has been beaten, and if she should be smashed, my father would order another."

I did not care so much about the boat as I did about the fellows in her. I did not wish to have even one of them drowned before my eyes. I put on my coat, and then pushed off from the wharf. In a few moments we were in the thickest of it, and even the Belle courtesied so low as to take in the "drink" over her lee rail. But I eased her off so that she went along very well, as any boat will when properly handled.

"They are hoisting sail," said Waddie.

"So much the worse for them," I replied.

"Have they reefed her?"

"I don't think they know enough to do that."

"They have! What are you going to do?"

"I am going to keep near enough to them to pull them out of the water if they get overboard."

"They are running right before the wind towards the Gulfport point. I think they have had sailing enough for one day. Let her out a little, Wolf; perhaps we can ascertain who they are."

"I think not. They will keep their faces covered up while you are around; for being found out would be almost as bad as being drowned to them."

The ruffians, probably seeing the sail on the Belle reefed, found that they could do a similiar thing with their own canvas. They had fastened the reef-points in some manner, and were running before the gale towards the rocky point. I did not understand what they intended to do; but it did not occur to me that they would be stupid enough to attempt a landing on a lee shore, in such a sea as raged at the time. If they had any common sense, it ought to have taught them better.

I let out the sheet, and gave chase. The Belle leaped like a race-horse over the waves, tossing the spray in bucketfuls over Waddie and myself. I hoped to overhaul the Highflyer — for that was the name of the other boat — in season to warn the ruffians of their danger. But they were half a mile to leeward of me when the chase commenced, for I did not think of pursuing them till they began to hoist the sail. I thought it would be time enough to help them when they called for assistance, as I was not quite sure they would not still subject my companion to further indignities if they could catch him on shore.

I was gaining rapidly on the Highflyer, under her clumsy management, and if there had been half a mile farther to run, I should have come up with her. The rascals in charge of her appeared to be profiting by their experience. They were daring fellows, as their intentions towards Waddie at the grove fully demonstrated, and they did not exhibit any signs of fear, though I could well believe they were not a little anxious about the future. Probably they had discovered that the Highflyer was a life boat, for her copper air-tanks were in plain sight, in her forward cuddy. To my mind it was a pity that such bold fellows should be such consummate rascals, for so I must call any persons who would tar and feather a boy, under any circumstances.

"What do you suppose they mean to do, Wolf?" asked Waddie, beginning to be much excited by the situation.

"I think they intended to go up to Centreport in your boat, but found they could not go against the wind. They didn't know how to beat her up. I believe they intend to get ashore now as quick as they can."

"Do they mean to land on those rocks ahead of them?"

"I should judge that they did.   They are not far from them, either," I replied.

"I may as well say good by to the Highflyer, then."

"I shouldn't wonder if you might say good by to some of those fellows also," I added, very anxious for the result.

Waddie said no more, and I did not then.   Both of us were bracing our nerves for the catastrophe, which could not be postponed many minutes longer.

"Boat, ahoy!" I shouted, with all the voice I could command.

"What do you want?" replied the gruff-toned fellow, who, in the boat as on the shore, was the leading spirit.

"Keep off the shore, or you will all be drowned!" I shouted.

"No, you don't!" answered back the chief conspirator.

This reply, being interpreted, evidently signified that the speaker did not mean to be caught or run down, or in any other way vanquished by his pursuer.

"By the great horn spoon," exclaimed Waddie, clinging to the side of the boat, "she is in for it!"

"Keep off!" I shouted, furiously; and by this time the Belle was within five rods of the Highflyer.

"Keep off yourself!" responded the gruff-toned fellow; and I noticed they had all covered their faces again.

"You will lose your lives if you don't keep off!" I added, with all the energy I could throw into the words.

I found it necessary, at this exciting point of the chase, to sheer off myself, lest a treacherous rock should knock a hole in the Belle. At the same instant the Highflyer rose on a wave, and then went down on the sharp rocks, with so much force that her bottom must have been completely stove in. I heard the crash, and held my breath with anxiety for the fate of the boys on board. They dropped down into the water, which I could now see rose within her nearly to the gunwales, and held on for life.

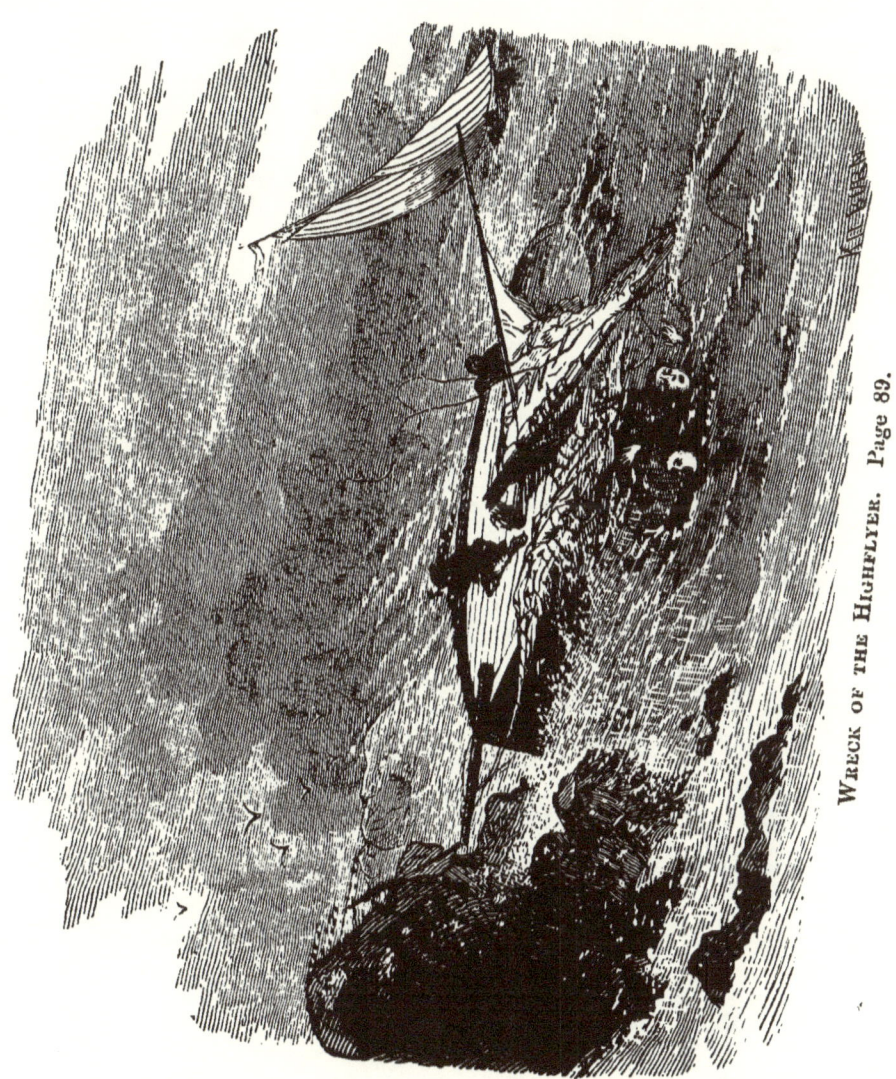

WRECK OF THE HIGHFLYER.   Page 89.

The receding wave carried the wreck back, and another lifted it up and jammed it down upon the jagged rocks with tremendous force. It was built of light material, and could not resist such a pounding for a single instant. Her mast went by the board, and she actually broke into pieces. The next wave that swept over her forced two of the four boys out of her, and pitched them into the water, while the other two held on to the fragments.

"That's rough!" gasped Waddie.

"I hope they will get out of it; but we can't do anything for them," I replied, with my heart in my throat.

I saw the two fellows who had been pitched out of the boat making their way over the rocks to the dry land. One of them limped, as though he had been severely injured. By this time all of them had lost their masks, or uncovered their faces; but they were too far from me to be identified. The Belle was now standing away from the scene of the thrilling event close-hauled; but we watched the two boys on the wreck, still fearful that the fierce waves might swallow them up. The billows continued to drive the fragments nearer to the shore, till we saw the boys rush through the water, and make their escape.

"That is the end of the Highflyer," said Waddie. I was thankful that it was not also the end of her late crew.

CHAPTER IX.

BY THE GREAT HORN SPOON!

BY this time the wind had increased to a tempest, and never before had I seen such waves and such spray on Lake Ucayga. I should not have been willing to believe that any sea that ever raged on our beautiful sheet of water could make such a complete wreck of a boat, even with the aid of the rocks, as that we had just witnessed. The High-flyer was as thoroughly broken up as though the work had been accomplished with axes and hammers, and the pieces were driven far up on the rocky shore.

The persecutors of Waddie had escaped; but they had probably been as effectually frightened as any four boys ever were before; and they were not likely to go into the business of navigation again on their own account very soon. They deserved a severe punishment; but on the whole, I was rather glad that we had not been able to identify them, for the vengeance of Waddie and his father was also so disproportionate to the offence, that, in the present instance, nothing less than the absolute ruin of the ruffians, and even of their families and friends, would appease the wrath of the injured magnate and his son.

The Belle behaved remarkably well. I was aware of her stiff and stanch character before I bought her; but she more than realized my expectations. She was as buoyant as a feather, and lifted her head to the seas as gracefully as though the tempest were her natural element. She took in torrents of spray, but she did not ship any water. Her mast bent like a reed in the blast, and of course I had to favor her when the heavy gusts struck her. Both Waddie and myself were wet to the skin, and both of us were shivering with the cold. It was not exactly pleasant, therefore, however exciting it was.

I ran the Belle out into the lake, and then at a single stretch made the pier at the picnic grove, the point from which we had started before. I was afraid I should lose my mast, and I was not disposed to cripple the boat merely to see what she could do. Behind the pier we had tolerably smooth water, and I decided to put another reef in the mainsail.

"What are you going to do now, Wolf?" asked Waddie, his teeth chattering as he spoke.

"I'm going to put in one more reef, for I don't like to risk my mast," I replied.

"Are you going to try to run down in the teeth of this blow?" he inquired.

"I must get home myself, and get the boat home."

"I thought you ran in here to wait for better weather."

"No; only to put in another reef."

"But I don't know that I can quite stand this. I am not afraid of anything, but I am half frozen."

"I'll warm you very soon, and you may go home as comfortably as though you were in the cabin of the Ucayga," I replied. "We are in no particular hurry, but I don't think we shall see any better weather to-day."

I went into the cabin, and lighted the fire in the little stove, which was filled with kindling wood ready for the match. I rigged the little copper funnel on the forward deck, and in that wind the draught was so strong that the fire roared merrily in a few moments. Having secured the mainsail, I joined Waddie in the cabin, closing the doors behind me. In less than half an hour we had a temperature of at least ninety degrees, and both of us were thawed out. We took off our coats, and placed them near the stove. We were as warm as toast, and though I did not announce the fact, I believed that the Belle was a great institution.

"I had something to eat on board of the High-flyer," said Waddie; "but my dinner has gone to destruction with the boat."

"I have some provisions on board, such as they are; but I suppose they will not suit one who sits at your father's table."

"Anything will suit me, Wolf. I am not dainty when I'm hungry; and I am as hungry as a bear."

"Well, I'm as hungry as a wolf."

"I suppose you are!" laughed Waddie, who appeared to be conscious that I had made a pun, though I did not regard it as a very savage one.

I took from the locker under the berth on which I sat a basket of " provender," which my mother had put up for me. For common sort of people I thought we lived very well, and I was not ashamed to produce the contents of my basket even in the presence of the little magnate of Centreport. I had some slices of cold ham, some bread and butter, and an apple pie. If the crust of the latter was a little coarse and dark-colored, it was still tender and healthful. I lowered the table, and arranged the food upon it, using the dishes which constituted a portion of the boat's furniture.

Waddie did me the honor to say that my dinner was quite as good, if not better than that which he had lost in the Highflyer, and he soon proved his sincerity by eating a quantity which rather astonished me, liberal feeder as I was. I am sure I relished the meal all the more because he enjoyed it so much. I should have added hot coffee to the feast, only we had no milk, and both of us agreed that coffee would not be coffee without this important addition.

The dinner was finished. I cleared away the dishes,

and restored the cabin to its usual order. By this time we were quite dry, for an atmosphere of from ninety to a hundred makes sharp warfare upon moist garments. The heat was beginning to be oppressive to me, and I opened the slide a little way to admit the fresh air, so abundant that day on the lake. I took my coat, and resumed my seat on the berth, for the cabin was not high enough to permit a standing posture. Waddie sat opposite to me. He had been in deep thought for some minutes, while I was making my preparations to breast the storm again.

I had put on my coat, and was buttoning it close around my throat, to keep out the cold and the water, when my companion startled me by a demonstration as strange in him as it would have been in the Emperor Napoleon, if I had been admitted to the sacred precincts of the Tuileries. Suddenly he sprang forward, and reached out his right hand to me across the table. I looked at it in bewildered astonishment, and with a suspicion that Waddie had suddenly become insane.

"Will you take my hand, Wolf?" said he, in the mildest of tones.

"Certainly I will, if you desire it;" and I clasped the offered member.

"Wolf, I have been your enemy," said he, still retaining my hand. "I have hated you; I have used you meanly; I have despised you. Will you forgive me?"

"With all my heart, Waddie," I replied, pressing his hand. "I never laid up anything against you."

"Are we friends?" he asked, earnestly.

"We are."

"By the great horn spoon, Wolf, I shall stick to you now like a brother! O, I'm in earnest, Wolf. You needn't smile at it!"

"I think you are sincere."

"I know I am. It is not altogether because you got me out of a bad scrape to-day that I say all this, but because you behaved so handsomely after all my meanness towards you. I don't understand it yet, Wolf. I don't see how you could do it; but I know it is so, and that's enough for me. I wish I could be like you."

"I hope you will be better than I am," I modestly replied.

7

"I don't ask to be any better than you are. All the fellows like you — I mean all the decent fellows. My father is rich, and yours is poor; but that don't seem to make any difference. The fellows on the other side would have mobbed Tommy Toppleton for your sake, if he hadn't broken his leg. I don't see why they should like you so much better than Tommy. Our fellows don't seem to like me much better, though I don't see why they shouldn't."

"Perhaps we will talk that over another time," I answered, not deeming it prudent to be entirely candid with him.

"I'm going to stick to you, Wolf, till the end of time, and I'm going to take your advice, too, if you will give it to me."

"I don't know that my advice will be worth much; but if I can be of any service to you, Waddie, I shall be very glad. I think we must get under way now."

"What shall I do?"

"Nothing at all. Stay in the cabin, and make yourself as comfortable as possible. I can handle the Belle without any assistance."

"But I want to talk with you some more."

"Well, we shall have time enough when we get down to Centreport."

"I feel as though you had been the best friend I ever had in the world, and, by the great horn spoon, I am going to be such a friend as you never had before."

"I wouldn't make any rash promises, Waddie," I answered, smiling at his enthusiasm. "You had better sleep on it."

"I don't want to sleep on it. I have been your enemy, but now I am your friend. If it hadn't been for me, you would have been running the Ucayga to-day."

"I don't find any fault, though such a berth as that would have suited me first rate," I continued, laughing; but I confess I had but little confidence in my new-made friend's zeal in my favor.

"It is not too late, Wolf, for my father and I are disgusted with the management of the boat, and it is high time something should be done."

"We will talk it over by and by," I added, leaving the cabin.

I put another reef into the mainsail, cast off the painter, which I had made fast to the pier, and pushed off. In a moment the Belle was rolling and pitching in the heavy surges of the lake. With two reefs in her mainsail she would not lie very close to the wind; but I ran her across the lake, intending to work along under the lee of the west shore, partially sheltered by the high bank from the fury of the tempest.

CHAPTER X.

WADDIE WIMPLETON IN A NEW CHARACTER.

EVEN as close-hauled as she could be under the double-reefed mainsail, the Belle flew on her course; but under this short sail she did not labor so heavily as before, and I had no fear but that she would make tolerably good weather of it. As I had anticipated, I found comparatively smooth water under the lee of the west shore; but, with two reefs in the mainsail, I found it impossible to lie close enough to the wind to avoid running out into the heavy sea.

I decided to make a sheltered cove, and turn out the last reef I had put in, satisfied that I could keep close enough under this sail to avoid the savage sea in the middle of the lake. Waddie was reclining upon one of the berths, as comfortable as though he had been in his father's house, while I was again

shivering with the cold, and wet to the skin. I supposed he was working up his good resolutions. I
never had much hope of Waddie, his temper was so
bad and his impulses so violent. On the other hand,
it had always seemed to me that a very little im-
provement would make a good fellow of Tommy
Toppleton. It was, therefore, almost incredible that
the former should be the first to proclaim his good
resolutions, and express a desire to mend his character.

Waddie's impulses, whether good or evil, appeared
to be equally violent. It is true I had never before
heard him whisper a doubt that he was not, even
morally, the best young man in the vicinity; but his
demonstration seemed to be rather too enthusiastic to
endure for more than a day or two, or a week at
the most. Tommy Toppleton had never, I confidently believe, soared to the elevation of making
good resolutions. If he had, there would have been
hope of him.

My companion in the boat was engaged in deep
and earnest thought. I should not have known any
better what he was thinking about if he had told me

in so many words. In the face of his earnestness, therefore, I could not help cherishing a slight hope that he would do better — it was not a strong hope. I determined to encourage him as much as I could, and in a gentle way, make such suggestions to him, from time to time, as his case seemed to require.

After all, it was not so surprising that Waddie should have his eyes opened by the exciting events of that day. He had been thoroughly convinced that he was not omnipotent; that there was such a thing as retribution. Probably he was also aware of the extent of the dislike with which the Wimpletonians regarded him. He was no fool, and ordinary perception would have enabled him to comprehend his relations with his associates at the Institute. I think he ought to have known all that Dick Bayard had told me; and possibly he was suspicious that his battalion, and the stockholders of his Steamboat Company intended to mutiny against him. At any rate, he was conscious of his own unpopularity; he had acknowledged as much to me. He was in deep thought. I did not disturb him.

I turned out the reef, and Waddie still devoted

himself to his meditations. The Belle filled away
again, and in the shelter of the shore went along quite
easily. The change in the motion of the boat seemed
to attract the attention of my passenger, and he
opened the slide to see what was going on.

"The wind has gone down — hasn't it, Wolf?"
said he.

"No; the sea is just as heavy out in the middle of
the lake as ever. We are under the lee of the shore
now."

"You seem to be quite comfortable. I think I will
come out, for I want to talk with you."

"It is pretty dry now. You will find some more old
coats under the port berth."

Waddie presently came out of the cabin, enveloped
in an old overcoat which my father had worn out.
He appeared to have something on his mind, of which
he was anxious to discharge himself. He took a seat
by my side; but, though the Belle was going along
tolerably well for such a day, he did not speak for
some time. Aware of his impulsive nature, I rather
expected to be appointed engineer or captain of the
Ucayga; for, as I have said before, he was the presi-

dent of the Steamboat Company, though his movements were more effectually controlled than his rival on the other side of the lake.

"Wolf, I know you don't like me very well," said he, at last, and with something like a troubled look on his face.

"Well, I can't say that your conduct towards me has been such as to make me love you very much. I won't be a hypocrite, Waddie," I replied.

"But what made you interfere when those fellows were abusing me?" he asked, looking me full in the face. "If you don't like me, why did you risk a broken head to save me? That's what I want to know."

"I don't know that I can explain my conduct very well," I answered, laughing. "I have always tried to think kindly of those who wanted to injure me. I thought that those fellows were doing an abominably mean and wicked thing, and that it was my duty to interfere. That's really all I know about it."

"I can't understand it. I was in hopes that, after all I have done and said, you really did like me."

"I don't dislike you."

"No matter; of course, I can't blame you for not liking me; but I want to begin anew. When I gave you my hand, and wanted to be friends, I was in real earnest. I want you to be my friend, and stand by me."

"Stand by you!" I exclaimed. "I can't stand by you unless you are in the right. I wouldn't stand by you, after you, with another, had caught a small boy, and licked him."

Waddie bit his lips, and I thought he was going to get mad, for what I had said was a home-thrust.

"I was wrong in that, Wolf," said he, with a struggle, which was creditable to him, and which raised him very much in my estimation.

"You were, indeed; and that scrape was the father of the one you got into to-day."

"I know it; and I am afraid there are other scrapes in store for me. The Institute fellows and the members of our battalion are down upon me; so is the Steamboat Company."

"Do you wish me to tell you just what I think, Waddie?" I asked.

"I certainly do."

"Even if it is not pleasant?"

"Yes; say on."

" If I were in your place, Waddie, I would be the most popular fellow in the whole region round about us. I would have every fellow like me, and stand by me," I continued, earnestly, as the boat approached the Narrows.

"Well, I have tried to be."

"Have you, indeed!" I replied, laughing in spite of myself at the absurdity of the proposition, though it is very likely Waddie believed what he said, strange as it may seem.

"I have been president of the Steamboat Company, major of the battalion; and I don't see why the fellows don't like me."

"I will tell you, candidly, why they do not. Because you think more of yourself than you do of any other fellow. You are selfish and exacting. You think every fellow ought to yield to you; and you are tyrannical and overbearing towards them. That's what's the matter, though I shouldn't have said so if you had not told me to do it."

"Do you think I am so bad as that?" said he, looking moody and solemn, rather than angry, as I supposed he would be.

"I have told you just what I think. Look at it for yourself a moment. Go back to the time when you blowed up that canal boat. Do you think you treated the skipper and his daughter just right? Then you threatened to blow out my brains if I did not do as you told me."

"Don't say any more about that. I am willing to own that I was wrong," pleaded he.

" Well, come down to a later day. At the auction, you commanded me not to bid on the Belle. You pitched into me, tooth and nail, because I did bid. You forbade my going on the Ucayga, just as Tommy Toppleton ordered me not to ride on his railroad, though I paid my fare in both instances. I don't rake up these things for any other purpose than to prove what I said. You can't expect any fellow to like you if you conduct yourself in this manner."

"What shall I do?"

"Do anything but what you have done. Respect the wishes and feelings, and especially the rights, of others, whether they be poor or rich. I happen to

know myself that the Institute fellows are down upon
you, and that they don't mean to stand your domineering and tyranny much longer."

"What are they going to do?" he asked, curiously.

"I'm sure I don't know; only that they mean
mutiny, in general terms. It is just the same on
our side of the lake. The Toppletonians intend to
pull Tommy down from his high places. At the last
election of officers they did elect another president,
but he declined to serve, though he was sorry enough
afterwards that he did not stand."

"You talk plainly, Wolf," continued Waddie, seriously. "I don't think I'm quite so hard a fellow as
you make me out to be."

"I tell you just what I think, and just what others
think."

"You are my friend now — are you not, Wolf?"

"I will do everything I can for you; and if you
will do what is right, I will stand by you to the end
of time."

"By the great horn spoon, I will do right if I know
how! You shall tell we what to do."

"I don't want to tell you what to do. If you mean
right, you can't very well go wrong."

"You will advise me — won't you?"

"Certainly I will, if you wish me to do so."

"What would you do now, if you were in my place?"

The arrival of the Belle at Centreport pier prevented me from answering this question, though I kept thinking of it while I was securing the boat to enable Waddie to go on shore. But he was not willing to part with me, and insisted so strongly that I should go up to "his house" with him, that I could not refuse. He clung to me like a brother, and I was confident that he intended then to mend his manners, whether he held out in the resolution or not. I lowered my sail, and walked up the street with him.

I went to his house, and the visit was productive of the most important results.

CHAPTER XI.

A STEAMBOAT STRIKE.

WHILE I was walking with Waddie from the pier to his father's house, I deemed it necessary to ask myself whether or not I was "toadying" to the son of the rich man of Centreport. I should have despised myself if I had believed such was the case. Both my father and myself were determined to be independent, in the true sense of the word. We had discussed the meaning of the word, and reached the conclusion that genuine independence was not impudence, a desire to provoke a quarrel, or anything of this kind. We agreed that the term was often misunderstood and abused.

But true independence was a genuine self-respect, which would not allow its possessor to cringe before the mighty, or to sacrifice honor and integrity for the sake of money or position. Doubtless both of us had been guilty, to some extent, of this subserviency; but we were determined not to fall below our standard again. Colonel Wimpleton and Major Toppleton had money and influence; but we had skill and labor. We could do without them quite as well as they could do without us. Avoiding all conspiracies, all impudence, and all intentions to quarrel, we meant to maintain our own self-respect. If neither of the great men wanted us, we could go elsewhere, and "paddle our own canoe" to our own satisfaction.

"I may say that my father and I had made a kind of compact of this nature; and when I found myself, to my great astonishment, and almost to my chagrin, to be hand and glove with Waddie, I began to suspect that I had been sacrificing myself to the mammon of influence. But a little reflection assured me I was not guilty of the charge. I had saved my new friend from a disgraceful and humiliating ordeal only from a sense of duty, and not with the intention of "currying favor" with him. I had told him, fairly and square-ly, what I thought of him, and what others thought of him. As I considered what I had said to him, I found no occasion to reproach myself. On the contrary, so far as appearances went, I had converted Waddie from the error of his ways.

My companion was gentle and kind to me. He acted like an altered person — using no harsh or bullying language, and appearing to be only anxious to ascertain what was right in order that he might do it. I followed him into his father's library, where a cheerful fire blazed in the grate, and we seated ourselves before it. I had hardly ever been in this room before, though I had frequently visited the major's library.

"Wolf, just as the Belle came up to the pier, I asked what you would do, if you were in my place," said Waddie, after we had comfortably disposed ourselves in the cushioned arm-chairs. "You did not answer me."

"You ask me hard questions, Waddie," I replied, laughing. "I do know what I should do if I were in your place, but I do not like to set myself up as your adviser."

"I ask you to do it. I will thank you for it."

"I will tell you what I think, and then you can do as you like. I can give you advice; but you are not obliged to follow it, you know."

8

"Don't you be so afraid to speak, Wolf!" added Waddie, rather impatiently.

" Well, then, in the first place, I should make my peace with all the fellows, whether in the Institute or not."

"I'm going to do that; but the thing of it is, how to do it."

" You have been riding a high horse. You are major, president, and I don't know what 'not. You have used those positions to tyrannize over and bully even your best friends."

" Well ? " said he, as I paused to note the effect of these words upon him.

" You must put yourself in a humble position, to begin with."

" I'll do it! By the great horn spoon, I'll do it!" exclaimed he, with enthusiasm. "I'll do anything you say, if it is to go down on my knees before the ragged little rowdies in the streets of Centreport."

" I shall not advise you to do anything of that kind; but, under the circumstances, I should resign the positions of major and president."

" Resign them!"

"Yes; I would show the fellows, first, that I am as willing .to obey as I am to command. The fellows mean mutiny, both in the Steamboat Company and in the battalion."

"I'll do it. What next?" he asked, rubbing his hands, in humble imitation of his magnificent father, when he was pleased.

"I should take my place in the battalion as a private, do my duty faithfully, and obey my officers in every respect. As a stockholder in the company, I should behave modestly, and not attempt to carry my points by bullying, or any other unfair practices. In any and every capacity, if I had an opportunity to do a kindness to either friend or enemy, I should do it, even at some considerable personal sacrifice. But I don't wish to burden you with my opinions."

"I thought you would tell me to go to the Sunday school, or something of that sort."

"I certainly recommend that; but I was speaking only of your relations with the boys in the vicinity. If you have a good heart, you will do your duty."

"There will be a meeting of the Steamboat Company next week. I will have my resignation ready.

O, I am in earnest — by the great horn spoon I am!" protested Waddie.

"Perhaps you had better consult your father. I don't want you to act blindly on my advice. He may not think it best for you to do as I say."

"I know he won't; and for that reason I shall not say anything to him. I'm not going to say anything against my father; but I know what's what."

"But you may endanger his interests in the steamer," I suggested.

"No; the directors can't do anything without his approval. There is no danger. Besides, my father is as cross as a bear lately. The railroad on the other side is beating us every day. He has been quarrelling with the captain and engineer for a week."

"Is it their fault that the boat is beaten?" I inquired.

"Father thinks it is, in part. The engineer won't drive the boat, and the captain is a slow coach."

Waddie had scarcely made his explanation before the library door opened, and Colonel Wimpleton bolted into the room. He appeared to be much excited, threw down his hat, and seemed to be disposed to smash things. He did not see me at first; but when he discovered my presence, he came up to me, and, to my great astonishment, offered me his hand. He glanced curiously at Waddie, as he realized the fact that his son was on good terms with me.

"I'm glad to see you, Wolf," said he, as he grasped my hand. "I suppose you thought I had forgotten you; but I have not. A Wimpleton never forgets a friendly act, nor forgives a malicious one. What's up, Waddie?" he continued, as he turned to his son.

"Wolf and I are the best friends in the world, father, replied Waddie. "Ain't we, Wolf?"

"That's so, just now; and I hope it will always continue," I replied.

"O, it will!" persisted Waddie.

"It's rather odd, to say the least," added the colonel, with an incredulous stare at both of us.

"I'll tell you how it happened," said Waddie.

And he related the history of the events of the morning, and gave me all the credit, and rather more, I thought, than I deserved.

"That was handsome of you, Wolf, after all that has happened. But who were these rascals? I will make an end of them!"

"We didn't know who they were; and we couldn't find out."

"I shall find out!"

Perhaps he would; but at that moment the captain and engineer of the Ucayga were announced, and the colonel began to look as savage as when he entered the room. The servant was told to admit them.

"The villains!" gasped the great man. "They were half an hour behind time this morning, though they did not wait for the up-lake boats."

"Perhaps they were not to blame, father," suggested Waddie, mildly.

"Not to blame! Do you think I don't know?"

The two men entered the library, hat in hand. They were brothers, which, perhaps, is the only explanation which can be offered of the fact that they adhered to each other in the present difficulty.

"Colonel Wimpleton, we came up to say that we have concluded not to run in the Ucayga any longer," said the captain, with considerable deference, though there was a kind of dogged firmness in his tones and in his looks.

"Well, sir!" snapped the colonel.

"We have done our best, but we can't please you."

"You can't please me *by* being half an hour behind time every day."

"It isn't my fault," protested the captain. "And I won't be insulted, as I have been to-day before all my passengers. You may get a new captain and a new engineer as soon as you please."

"None of your impudence!"

"My impudence is no worse than yours. You won't find any men who can do better than we have."

"If I can't I will sink the boat in the middle of the lake."

"We don't want to talk; our time is out."

"Don't you mean to run the trip this afternoon?" demanded the colonel, whose face suddenly flushed, as he saw the trick of his employees.

"No, sir! We do not," replied the captain, a gleam of satisfaction on his face, as he realized that he was punishing the great man.

"Don't say a word, father. Let them go," whispered Waddie.

" You will find that we are not slaves," added the captain.

Colonel Wimpleton looked at his watch. It wanted only half an hour of the advertised time to start the boat for Ucayga. He looked at Waddie, looked at me, and then at the two men, who doubtless expected, by the means they had chosen, to bring him down from "the high horse." I watched the great man with intense interest; and perhaps I was as much excited as any person in the room.

CHAPTFR XII.

CAPTAIN WOLF PENNIMAN.

MY impression now is, that neither the captain nor the engineer really intended to throw up his situation. While I could not, and did not, blame them for refusing to submit to the savage abuse of Colonel Wimpleton, I did not think it was quite fair to spring this trap upon their employer within thirty minutes of the time the boat was to start. But the colonel was not altogether unreasonable in his complaints. The men did not use every exertion to be on time. There was fault on both sides.

The captain had been instructed not to lose his connection, even if he always went without the up-lake passengers. On this day, as I learned, he had failed to connect, though he had not waited for the Hitaca boat. Passengers were dissatisfied, and the new steamer was rapidly losing the favor of the travelling public.

Colonel Wimpleton, as he stood before the fire in his library, realized that these men were trying to punish him. The whispered words of Waddie evidently made their impression upon him. He curbed his wrath, and was silent for a moment.

"Let them go, father," said Waddie.

He did let them go, and gave them an order on his agent for their wages.

"Will the boat make her trip this afternoon?" asked the captain, who did not seem to be pleased with the result of the interview.

"That's my affair," replied the colonel.

"We are going on board for our things. We have steam up, and if she is not going, my brother will have the fires raked down."

"He needn't trouble himself. You have an order for your money — good afternoon."

The two men took this hint and left.

"By the great horn spoon!" shouted Waddie, springing to his feet.

"What's to be done?" queried the colonel, glancing at me.

"Wolf, you are the captain of the Ucayga from this

moment!" roared Waddie, slapping me furiously on the back. "This is my last act as president of the Steamboat Company! Do you approve it, father?"

"It is what I wanted before. But we have only half an hour — less than that," replied the great man, looking at his watch again.

"We can make time if we are fifteen minutes late. Do you accept, Wolf?"

"I do; with many thanks."

"But the engineer?" said the colonel, anxiously.

"Send over for my father with all possible haste. I will go down and look out for the engine until he comes," I replied.

"I will go over myself in your boat, Wolf. In this breeze I can cross in five minutes," added Waddie, seizing his hat, and rushing out of the house.

"I will go with you to the steamer, Wolf," said Colonel Wimpleton.

All this was so sudden that I had not time to realize the situation. As I walked down to the wharf with the magnate of Centreport, I recalled some mysterious words of Waddie, which seemed now to have a point. He had told me that I should not care to go up the lake the next week with the fishing party. Certainly he could not have known that the event which had just occurred would open the way for me; but he was doubtless aware that the moment he said the word the captain of the Ucayga would be discharged. He knew that his father was dissatisfied with the management of the boat, and I suppose, as soon as he had determined to be my friend, he meant to give me the position.

"Wolf, I have intended this place for you ever since you used me so well in the yacht," said the colonel, as we walked down the street. "Waddie would not consent. He hated you like a demon. But you have conquered him, and that is more than I could ever do."

I wanted to tell him that good was all-powerful against evil; but the remark looked egotistical to me, and I suppressed it.

"I hope you don't expect too much of me." I replied.

"No; but I expect a good deal of you. Everybody on the lake knows you; and you are smart. We must beat that railroad some how or other."

"I think we can, sir, if we have any kind of fair play. But Major Toppleton's boats are always ten or fifteen minutes behind time."

"No matter if they are. If you leave at half past two, you can always make time, if you don't waste your minutes, as our captain often has done. Wolf, I believe he has been bribed by Toppleton to lose his connections."

"I don't know about that."

"He is a Hitaca man, and has no sympathy with our side of the lake."

Perhaps the colonel was right. When I looked the matter over afterwards, I was satisfied that there was some ground for the suspicion. We reached the wharf, and went on board of the Ucayga. We arrived at just the right time, for both the captain and the engineer were stirring up ill feeling among the crew of the boat; and the latter was at work on the engine, with the evident intention of spoiling the afternoon trip. Colonel Wimpleton drove them ashore without indulging in any unnecessary gentleness. I directed the fireman to fill up the furnaces, and overhauled the machinery. While I was thus engaged, my father arrived.   He was conducted to the engine-room by Waddie.

"Mr. Penniman, allow me to introduce you to Captain Penniman, master of the steamer Ucayga," said the president of the Steamboat Company, with a degree of good-nature of which I had never before supposed him capable.

"Captain Penniman, I am happy to make your acquaintance," laughed my father, as he grasped my hand, and gave it a significant pressure. "I think our family is getting up in the world, for we have now the honor to boast that we have a steamboat captain in it."

"A very great honor, no doubt; but it will depend somewhat upon the manner in which he discharges his duties," I replied, as good-naturedly as either of my companions. "Father, we are on duty now, and we must be on time."

I looked at my watch.   It still wanted ten minutes of half past two. Waddie had been so fortunate as to find my father on the wharf, and had not been delayed a moment in procuring his services. While at work on the engine I had been making a close calculation. It was necessary to land our passengers on the wharf at Ucayga by four o'clock, which gave me an hour and a half to make the distance, — twenty miles, — including the stay in Ruoara, generally of fifteen minutes.

My predecessor, when he left the wharf in Centreport at half past eight in the forenoon, or half past two in the afternoon, was pretty sure to miss his connection; but he had gone over twenty-one miles, while I intended to save more than a mile, equivalent to five minutes of time, in the passage. I had thought over this matter before, and though my appointment had been sudden, I was not unprepared for my difficult and delicate task.

"Father, great things are expected of us," said I, as Waddie went out of the engine-room to witness the arrival of the old Ruoara, which was just then coming in at the other side of the wharf.

"I trust we shall not disappoint them; but I hope you know what you are about," replied he, casting an anxious glance at me.

"I do, father; I am just as confident as though I had been running this boat for a year. I want you to run her at the highest speed you can with safety."

"I will do it. I served my time on a steamer, and I am at home here."

"Keep her moving lively; that's all I want," I replied, as I left the engine-room, and made my way to the hurricane deck.

Colonel Wimpleton had employed a couple of "runners" properly to set forth to the passengers who were going through, the merits of his new and splendid steamer. They were duly posted up in the change which had just been made.

"Take the Ucayga, Captain Wolf Penniman!" shouted these worthies. "Sure connection! No failure this time! You have to change three times by the railroad. The Ucayga, Captain Wolf Penniman, gentlemen!"

I was rather startled to hear my name thus freely used; but I was surprised and gratified to see that not a few of the passengers came on board of the steamer, though they were told by the railroad runners that they would be sure to miss the train at Ucayga. I recognized not a few of those whom I had known on

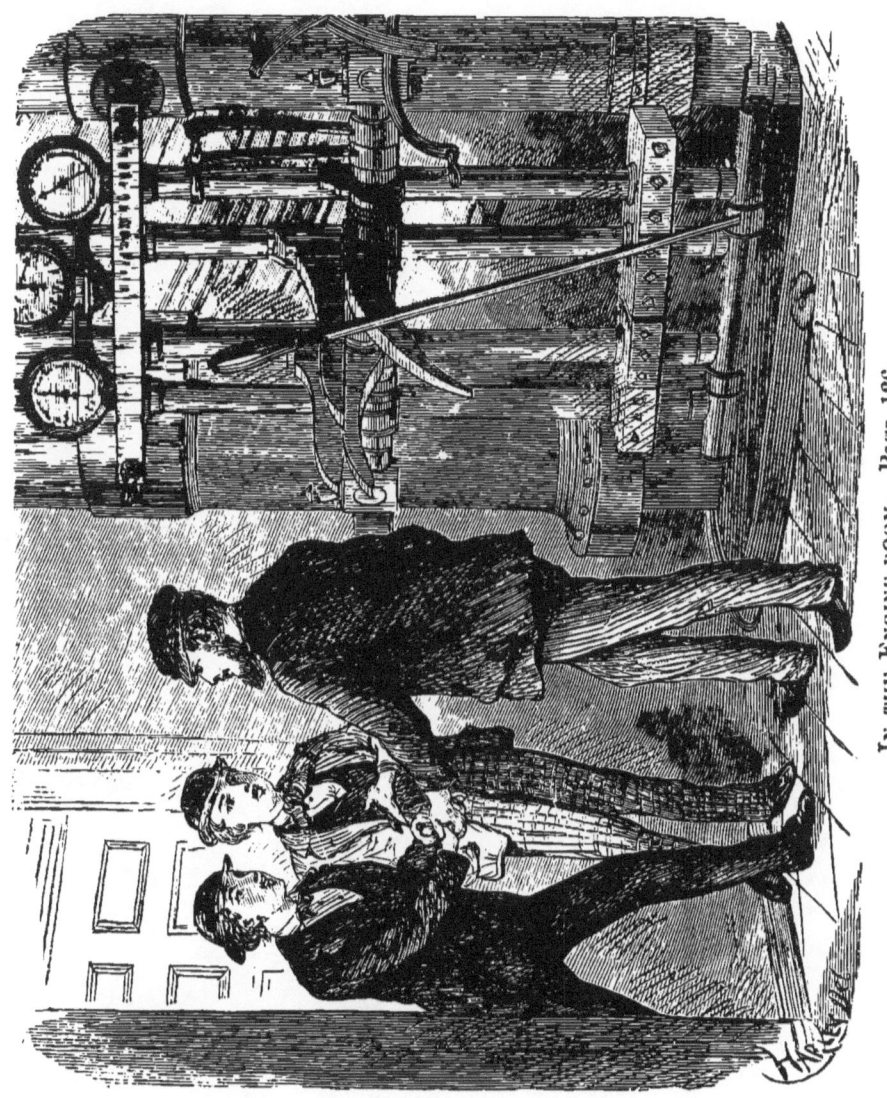

IN THE ENGINE-ROOM. Page 126.

the railroad, persons who had come to the engine to talk with me, while waiting for the train or the boat.

" All aboard that's going!" shouted the mate of the Ucayga.

" Haul in the planks, and cast off the fasts," I called to the hands who were in readiness to discharge this duty.

I confess that my bosom thrilled with strange emotions as I issued my first order. But I felt quite at home, for I had run a great deal upon the old boats, both in the engine-room and on deck. I had witnessed the operation of making a landing so frequently, that I was sure I could do it without assistance, if necessary. I had measured the distance, estimated the force of winds and currents, so many times, that I had thoroughly conquered the problem.

The Ruoara backed out and headed for Middleport at quarter of three, for the train started at three. Lewis Holgate still ran the locomotive, and it had been found that he must start on time or he was sure to miss his connection.

No regular pilots were employed on any of these steamers. The mate and deck hands took the wheel

9

when required, and any of them were able to make the landing. I told the former to take the wheel, for I had decided to let him make the landings on this trip, rather than run even the slightest risks by my own inexperience. The Ucayga slipped out from the wharf, and my father, true to his instructions, gave her full steam.

"We are nearly ten minutes later than usual," said Colonel Wimpleton, shaking his head ominously, as we met on the forward deck.

"I pledge you my word, sir, that the boat shall be in Ucayga on time," I replied, confidently.

CHAPTER XIII.

IN THE WHEEL-HOUSE.

COLONEL WIMPLETON was evidently very anxious, as he had been from the beginning, for the success of the steamer. On the present occasion, when the Ucayga was nearly ten minutes behind her ordinary time, I grant that he had not much to hope for in the light of past experience; but he did not know my plans, and I did not wish to startle him by announcing them, fearful that, if I did so, he would not permit me to carry them out. I repeated my promise to be on time, and though he was far from satisfied, he could not do anything but wait the result.

My calculations were based upon the assured fact that the Ucayga could easily make sixteen miles an hour. She had the reputation of being a fast boat, and I intended that she should sustain her reputation.

Immense expense had been lavished upon her to give her great speed, as well as to make her elegant and commodious. The testimony was, that she had repeatedly made her sixteen miles without straining or undue crowding. This was all I asked of her. If she did only what she was warranted to do, and what she had often accomplished, I was safe.

I knew every tree and point on the west shore, along which the railroad extended, and its exact distance from Middleport. I watched these points, and consulted my watch frequently, to assure myself that the boat was not falling behind my calculations. Her first four miles were made inside of fifteen minutes, and I was not sure that my father was not overdoing the matter; but he was a safe man, and I did not think it necessary even to see him.

On the forward deck I attended to the arrangement of the baggage, so as to make the stay at Ruoara as brief as possible. There were two baggage trucks, upon which I caused to be loaded all the freight, luggage, and merchandise for Ruoara. I saw that the deck hands were rather disposed to snuff at a boy like me in command of the steamer; but, in self-defence, I must add that I was nearly as tall as a man. They were slow, and did not obey promptly. I thought I could in part explain the failure of my predecessor to be on time. But it was of no use for me to bluster at these men, though they were probably working more leisurely than usual.

"Is everything going to suit you?" asked the colonel, as they were approaching the wharf at Ruoara.

"Not quite, sir."

"What's the matter?" he demanded, anxiously.

"The men work as though they were digging their own graves, which were to be occupied as soon as finished."

"Don't they mind you?"

"They don't refuse to mind, but they are slow. They think I'm only a boy."

"I'll discharge every one of them!"

"Excuse me, sir, but don't do that. I would rather add a quarter a day to their wages," I replied; for I happened to know that they were greatly dissatisfied with their pay, and justly so, I thought. "Then, if they don't work, they shall be discharged."

"Do so, if you think best," replied the colonel, promptly.

"And the mate?"

"Give him half a dollar a day, if that will help the matter."

"I think they are not paid fair wages, or I would not have said a word. As it is, I can make friends of them in this way."

"Only beat the railroad, and I don't care what it costs," replied the magnate, impatiently.

"I will do it, sir."

The plan was a stroke of policy on my part. As a boy I could do nothing with these men by bullying and threatening them. By doing a good thing for them, I could conquer them easily. I went up to the wheel-house as the boat neared the wharf.

"Mr. Van Wolter, I will thank you to make this landing yourself," said I, addressing the mate, who had the wheel.

"I think I can do it," replied he, with a broad grin, which was as much as to say that I could not do it.

"So can I; but I prefer that you should do it this time," I added.

"I suppose so!" he answered, with something like a sneer. "The mate, on a dollar and a half a day, is always expected to do the captain's work on this boat."

"I shall not ask you to do mine; but are you dissatisfied with your wages?"

"I think the pay is mean."

"So do I; and from to-day your wages shall be two dollars a day. I have already spoken to Colonel Wimpleton about this matter, and he consents to it."

"Thank you; that's handsome," replied Van Wolter. "Excuse me for what I said just now; I didn't mean anything by it."

"All right. I want you to have the boat ready to start in just seven minutes after she stops at the wharf. And to help the matter, you may say to the hands, that their pay shall be raised a quarter of a dollar each per day. They must work lively when we make a landing."

"You are a gentleman and a scholar, Captain Penniman, and what you need most time will give you."

"What's that?"

"More years."

He rang the bell, slowed the boat, and made as beautiful a landing as I had ever seen in my life. The moment the steamer touched the wharf, he rushed down the ladder to the forward deck.

"Now, lively, my men!" shouted he, as he grasped the handles of one of the trunks.

I saw him say something, in a low tone, to the hands. I knew what it was, and the effect was electrical. They worked well, and tumbled in the freight with an alacrity which must have astonished the staid citizens of that place who had gathered on the wharf. It was Saturday, and there was a large quantity of freight, and a great many passengers; but within the seven minutes I had named, the steamer was ready to be off. I had saved half the time usually taken up in this landing, and there was room to reduce it still more.

"You are late again," said a gentleman to Colonel Wimpleton, as he came on board. "We shall lose the train."

"I hope not."

"O, I know we shall. I think our people will have to go over to Grass Springs and take the train."

"We shall be on time, sir," I ventured to say.

"I think we shall," added the colonel.

"All aboard, and all ashore!" shouted the mate,

with a zeal born of the half dollar per day his pay had been increased.

I sprang up the ladder, and took my place in the wheel-house. It was just ten minutes past three. I was five minutes inside of my own calculations, but more than ten behind the steamer's usual time. "The tug of war" had come for me, for I intended to steer the boat myself, and save from five to ten minutes of the boat's ordinary time. I must now explain, more particularly than I have before done, how this feat was to be accomplished.

As I have before stated, the South Shoe lay off the town of Ruoara. It was exactly due west from the wharf where the Ucayga made her landing. To the southward and westward of this island the water was shallow, and more than a mile was added to the distance from Ruoara to Ucayga by going round these shoals, or about five minutes to the time. But this was not all. The boat was obliged to back, and actually turn, before she could go ahead at full speed; and this operation would consume all of five mintues more.

I have before spoken of the narrow passage between

the Horse Shoe and the Shooter, where the Toppletonians landed when they took possession of the former
island.   This channel was very narrow, but it was also
very deep.   I proposed to run the Ucayga through
this passage, and thus save ten minutes on the trip.
The steamer made her landing at the end of the wharf,
so that she did not have to turn; and all we had to do,
making the passage in the direction indicated, was to
cast off the fasts and go straight ahead.

Ruoara was built on a broad point of land which
projected out into the lake, so that the narrow channel
lay due north of the end of the pier.   A straight line
through the channel, as the needle points, would strike
the North Shoe; and this circumstance rendered the
navigation beyond the passage rather difficult.   But I
had thought of the problem so many times, that I was
satisfied, knowing the channel as well as I did, that I
could take the steamer through without any trouble.

"Cast off your fasts, and haul in the plank!" I
shouted from my position, as I grasped the wheel.

The zealous crew, inspired by the increase of their
wages, promptly obeyed the order.   I rang the bell to
go ahead, just as Van Wolter entered the wheel-house.

Perhaps my readers may not feel much confidence in my skill, and it may be necessary for me to repeat the statement that I had spent a great deal of time on board of the steamers on the lake, most of it in the engine-room with Christy Holgate, it is true, but not a little of it on deck and in the wheel-house. I had often steered the boat. I had found the helmsman was as willing to be relieved as my instructor, the engineer, had been. I knew the wheel, and I knew the bells. I rang to go ahead, and gave the wheel a sheer to port.

"You want to back her first — don't you?" suggested Van Wolter, in a very respectful tone.

"No; I'm going to show you what I can do now," I replied, with a smile.

"But, captain, you will be aground in three minutes," protested the mate, laying his hand on the wheel.

"Let me alone! Don't bother me now," I replied, rather sharply, as the steamer gathered headway.

I snapped the bell again, to go ahead full speed, and away she buzzed towards the narrow channel.

"I don't know about this!" exclaimed Van Wolter.

"I do; don't say a word."

He did not; but in half a minute more Colonel Wimpleton and Waddie both appeared at the door of the wheel-house, and rushed in, highly excited, and evidently expecting to be smashed in a couple of minutes.

"Where are you going, Wolf?" demanded the colonel, almost fiercely.

"To Ucayga, sir," I replied.

"Stop her, this instant!"

"Too late, now, sir. I'm all right; I know what I'm about," I answered.

The boat rushed into the narrow channel.

CHAPTER XIV.

THROUGH THE HORSE SHOE CHANNEL.

COLONEL WIMPLETON, Waddie, and the mate all held their breath as though they expected to see the magnificent Ucayga knocked in splinters the next instant. She was going at full speed through the narrow channel; but, if I had been underneath her, I could not have told any better how many feet and inches there were between her keel and the sands at the bottom of the channel. If the passage through this narrow place was thrilling to others, it was more so to me, and I was fully conscious of the responsibility that rested upon me.

If the steamer struck the ground it would be ruin to me. My new-found situation, and all the emoluments attached to it, would be lost. But I felt that a failure to be on time at Ucayga would be hardly less fatal to me. I had fought the battle faithfully for the Lake Shore Railroad, when I was in the employ of the company, and had never missed a train. I intended to be equally faithful and devoted to the Steamboat Company. I knew what was expected of me, and I was determined that my boat should always be on time.

Success was a duty. The first step towards a failure was to believe in one. I had figured up my plan so carefully that I knew what could be done, always providing that the steamer was up to her guaranty. I was thrilled by the situation; but I was confident and determined. I could not take my eye off the course for an instant to look at Colonel Wimpleton and his son; but I could judge of their suspense and anxiety by the breathless silence they maintained. If the Ucayga took the ground, I should hear from them then; and that would be as soon as I cared to have the spell broken.

I had not yet reached the most difficult point of the navigation. If I continued on my straight course, the steamer would strike on the North Shoe, and the problem to be practically solved was, whether the boat could be turned about forty-five degrees without being swept upon the shoals to the northward. She was a long vessel, and it required all the philosophy and science I possessed to meet the question. When the helm was put to starboard, the momentum of the steamer would tend to throw her course outside of the arc of the circle she would describe in turning. The faster she went the greater would be her momentum, or, after she had begun to turn, her centrifugal force.

I had studied a great deal over this question since I visited Ruoara to purchase the Belle, for I was convinced that this passage must be open to the boat in order to enable her to compete with the railroad, by saving at least ten minutes of precious time. I had studied it over very carefully, with every possible allowance for wind and current. I had chalked out diagrams of the channel on the ceiling boards of the Belle, and my policy was thoroughly defined in my own mind. The channel between the Horse Shoe and the North Shoe was perhaps a hundred and twenty feet wide — it did not vary twenty feet from this distance, I knew. When the boat was within a hundred feet of the bend in the channel, I rang to stop her.

"I thought you would have to back out," said Colonel Wimpleton, drawing a long breath, perhaps of relief to find that the magnificent craft was not already high and dry on the shoals.

"I'm not going to back out, sir — by no means," I replied, as I threw the wheel over to starboard.

The Ucayga surged ahead under the impetus she had attained, and turned her bow to the west, with the shoal close aboard of her on the port side. She minded her helm beautifully, and as soon as I had brought the bow flag-pole in range with the chimney of a certain cottage on the west shore, I rang to go ahead. Righting the helm, I let her go again at full speed. The allowance I had made for the centrifugal sweep of the boat carried me clear of the shoals on the starboard hand; and, though I had hugged the shoal on the port hand, the actual course of the boat was very nearly in the middle of the channel. In a couple of minutes more all danger had been passed.

"You may take the helm now, if you please, Mr. Van Wolter," said I to the mate.

"By the great horn spoon," roared Waddie, "we are out of that scrape!"

"That was done as handsomely as ever I saw any-thing done in my life!" exclaimed the mate, with a broad grin on his good-natured face.

"I don't know about that, Wolf," said the colonel, shaking his head, while the relief which he felt was plain enough upon his face.

"You know that we have saved ten minutes by that operation, sir," I replied, looking at my watch. "It is seventeen minutes past three, and we have only nine miles more to make, which can be done in thirty-five minutes. This will bring us in at the wharf at seven minutes before four. We shall have at least five min-utes to spare. We should certainly have been behind time if we had gone around the South Shoe."

"But do you think it is safe to go through that narrow place, Wolf?" asked the great man.

"I think I can take this boat through a thousand times without failing once," I answered, wiping the perspiration from my brow, for the intense excitement of the passage, overlooked and criticised as I was by the magnate and his son, had thrown me into a fever heat.

"If I had known what you intended to do, I would not have permitted it."

10

"For that reason, sir, I did not tell you," I replied, laughing. "I want to say, sir, that I haven't done this thing blindly and recklessly."

"That's so!" exclaimed the mate, who understood the matter better than any one present except myself.

"You said something to me a few weeks ago about taking command of this boat, Colonel Wimpleton. Well, sir, I have studied up this subject, and taken the shore bearings. I can give you the precise rule I followed."

"I should like to hear it," said the colonel, bestowing upon me a cheerful smile of approbation.

"Yes, sir. When the pine tree on the Shooter ranges with the barn on the east shore, stop her. Then, when the north point of the Shooter ranges with an oak tree on the east shore, starboard the helm. When the boat has turned so that the chimney of the cottage ranges with the bow flag-pole, the pilot sighting from the centre of the wheel-house, go ahead again. Then you are all right; and it can be done a thousand times without a single failure if you follow the directions."

"But why do you stop her?" asked the colonel, curiously.

"So that, in turning, the tendency to sweep too far to starboard may be counteracted in part. But after I have tried it a few times, I can go through without stopping her."

"You are a genius," laughed the colonel. "I begin to hope that we shall beat the railroad, after all."

"We are sure of it every time we can leave Centreport at two-thirty."

"The up-lake boats must get to Centreport as soon as that in order to enable the train to be on time," replied Colonel Wimpleton, rubbing his hands as though he was master of the situation.

"I don't think you are quite ready for Major Toppleton's next step," I replied, rather amused at his want of forethought.

"What do you mean by his next step?"

"The one I should take myself if I were in his place."

"What's that?"

"I think we are beating him just now, sir; and, as soon as the major finds out that we are getting ahead of him, he will make another move. We are sure of the Centreport and Ruoara trade, as long as

we are on time. He can't get that away from us.
But we want our share of the up-lake business."

"Yes, and we must have it," added the great man,
impatiently.

"Major Toppleton has bought up the stock of the
old line of boats, and runs them to favor the railroad.
The only possible motive he can have for sending his
boats to Centreport, is for the accommodation of passengers from Hitaca to that place. There are only a
few of them. His next step, then, will be to run his
boats only to Middleport, so that you shall not have
an opportunity to catch a single through passenger."

"That occurred to me," replied the colonel.

If it had occurred to him, he had been singularly
careless about providing a remedy.

"It will be done just as soon as the major sees
that we can make our trip from Centreport to Ucayga
in one hour and a half, including the stop at Ruoara.
I am satisfied you will see the posters announcing
a new arrangement within a week."

"I don't see that I can help myself," added the
magnate, biting his lips with vexation.

"Don't you, sir?"

"No, I do not," continued the colonel, opening his eyes.

"If you wish it, you can have the entire control of the travel on this lake. After you have made your next move, Major Toppleton and the railroad will be nowhere."

"I don't understand you, Wolf."

"You must build the mate to this steamer as soon as possible."

"That's rather a costly experiment," mused the great man."

"But it will pay, for you will have the entire travel on the lake, with the exception of the three towns on the railroad. The through travel pays the bills, and you can have all that. Those old boats make only ten miles an hour, and it takes them three hours, including stops, to come from Hitaca to Centreport. The Ucayga would make the distance in two. Your line can leave the head of the lake an hour later than the old line, and get to Ucayga in three hours and a half, while it will take the old line four hours and a quarter."

"You are right, Wolf!" exclaimed the colonel.

"I'll build another boat at once, and call her tho Hitica. Let me see you to-night, when you get in, and we will talk it over again."

The Ucayga was approaching the railroad wharf. The Lightning Express train was just coming in sight, at least ten minutes behind time. When my boat touched the wharf, it was just eight minutes of four.

CHAPTER XV.

A DECIDED VICTORY.

THE up-lake boat had arrived at Centreport rather later than usual. Certainly the Ucayga had left her wharf at full ten minutes behind her ordinary time. The steamer had had even a less favorable chance than before, and, under her former management, she must have been fifteen or twenty minutes behind time. I had saved at least five minutes of the stay at Ruoara, and ten more by going through the Horse Shoe Channel.

The two trains which met at Ucayga were due at five minutes of four. They were seldom more than five minutes behind time, and as they were both obliged to make connections, they could not wait many minutes for either boat or cars. "On Time," therefore, meant something; and it was an inexpressible pleasure to me that I had complied with the conditions. Boat stock would go up after this feat had been performed a few times, especially if the Lightning Express was, as on the present occasion, ten minutes late.

The steamer from Hitaca had arrived at Centreport at about half past two. She had left for Middleport as soon as she could take in and discharge her freight; but she must have been five minutes late for the express train. Lewis Holgate had probably wasted five minutes more. When the Ucayga was made fast at the wharf, the train had just reached the ferry on the other side of the river — the outlet of the lake. The trains east and west were on time, and by four o'clock, all the passengers who were going in them were in their seats. The ferry-boat had not yet started. The conductors stamped their feet, and looked at their watches every half minute. To wait for the Lightning Express passengers would add ten minutes more to the time to be made up in running about twenty-five miles.

As the boat on the other side did not start, the conductors decided not to wait any longer. The bells rang, and the two trains puffed, and snorted, and went on their way. I have no doubt there were many hard words used by the people on board of the ferry-boat, as they saw these trains start. If Major Toppleton was on board, I had no doubt he used some big words, for he was not above the infirmity of doing so when irritated.

Steamer stock went up, and railroad stock went down. In a fair competition, we had beaten the Lightning Express. I was satisfied that this calamity to the railroad, under the circumstances, would cost Lewis Holgate his situation; for the major, and even Tommy, would be indignant at the result. I was confident that what we had done this time could always be done, for we had made our quick time against a strong head wind.

"We have done it, Wolf!" exclaimed Waddie, as he came up to me, with a familiar slap on the back, after the trains left.

"Yes; and we have done it under rather unfavorable circumstances," I replied, quite as pleased as he was with the result.

"No matter, so long as we have done it. If we can only keep doing it, I shall be satisfied."

"We can; as long as we can leave Centreport at

half past eight in the morning, and half past two in the afternoon, I will guarantee to land the passengers here at five minutes before ten and five minutes before four. Of course some accident may happen once or twice a year, but the rule shall be without any ordinary exception."

"I wish we could compete with them going the other way," said Waddie, anxiously.

"I wish we could; but I don't think that will be practicable until we have another boat. With one more steamer, we can have it all our own way," I replied.

"Can't we do anything, Wolf?"

"If the up-lake boats will be ten or fifteen minutes late in leaving Centreport, we may; but we can't promise to land passengers there in season to continue their trip by the next boat. You must not promise anything which you are not sure of performing."

"I wish we could do something," added Waddie. "I would give anything to beat the railroad both ways."

"We can mend the matter; but I don't think we can always be sure of connecting with the Hitaca boat. Let us see. Our time table now is: —

Leave Ucayga, ... 4.15.

Arrive at Ruoara, ... 5.00.

Leave Ruoara, ... 5.15.

Arrive at Centreport, ... 5.45.

We can improve this, I think," said I, writing on a card the places and times as I stated them.

"Leave Ucayga, ... 4.00.

Arrive at Ruoara, ... 4.45.

Leave Ruoara, ... 4.55.

Arrive at Centreport, ... 5.25.

That is twenty minutes better than we do now."

"But the Hitaca boat is advertised to leave Centreport at 5.15," interposed Waddie, looking over my figures.

"She is advertised to do it, but lately she has been regularly ten or fifteen minutes behind time," I replied. "To-day she will be nearer half an hour."

"Try it on, Wolf," said Waddie, with enthusiasm.

"I will; but you must not go before your advertised hours."

"That will make no difference. We are advertised to go on the arrival of the boats and trains."

"Then what are we waiting for?" I replied. "All aboard!" I called to Van Wolter, the mate.

My zealous assistant shouted the usual warnings, and passengers on the wharf, who were waiting for the ferry-boat, were invited to come on board. Some of them accepted the assurance of Waddie that we should connect with the Hitaca boat at Centreport, and took passage with us. Just as the Middleport, with her indignant passengers, approached the wharf, the Ucayga backed out, and commenced her trip up the lake.

"You appear to be in a hurry, Wolf," said Colonel Wimpleton, taking a seat with me in the wheel-house, where Van Wolter had the helm.

I showed him the card on which I had written out the time I proposed to make.

"We can leave Ucayga at four o'clock as well as quarter of an hour later," I added. "The Lightning Express cannot land a passenger in Centreport in a minute less than an hour and a quarter. We can make our sailing time in just that space. If we can save five or ten minutes of our stay at Ruoara, we need not be more than five or ten minutes behind this time in reaching Centreport.

"Do as you think best, Wolf," replied Colonel Wimpleton, with the most friendly smile I had ever seen on his face.

" We shall get to Centreport first to-day, without a doubt."

We discussed the matter for a while, but we were satisfied that nothing more than a temporary advantage could be gained until we had another steamer. Before the Ucayga reached the islands I took a walk through the boat. Among the passengers I met quite a number whom I had known on the Lightning Express, and was very kindly congratulated upon my advancement. Some of them laughed at the idea of a boy like me commanding such a steamer; but I defended myself from the charge of being a boy. I should soon be seventeen; my mustache was beginning to develop itself, and I was only a few inches shorter than my father. Younger fellows than I had done bigger things than to command a lake steamer. I had shaved myself every week or fortnight for six months, borrowing my father's razor when he was away, and performing the operation in the secrecy of my chamber, with the door bolted, to prevent the possibility of an interruption, and the consequent annoyance of being twitted.

I made a desperate resolve, after being "bothered" for my juvenility, to purchase a razor and other implements, and shave myself every day, so as to encourage the downy growth upon my upper lip and chin. I also decided to have a frock-coat, and to wear a hat, in order still further to obviate the objectionable circumstances of "the young captain of the Ucayga steamer." I regarded it as rather malicious in people to insist upon it that I was a boy. I was not a boy. I was at least a young man, and I was doing a man's work. They might as well call a man of thirty a boy because he played base ball.

In my tour of inspection I called upon my father in the engine-room. I had not seen him since the boat left Centreport. Like a faithful engineer, he had looked only at the machinery before him, and not troubled himself about other matters. He hardly knew anything of the exciting events in which he had been a prominent actor.

"How goes it Wolf?" he asked, as I sat down in his arm-chair.

"First rate."

"Have you quarrelled with Waddie or the colonel yet?" he inquired, laughing.

"No, sir, and am not likely to do so at present. I

am not on the top of the wave. We have beaten the Lightning Express down, and are going to do the same thing up."

"Don't overdo the matter, and don't promise more than you can perform."

"I don't intend to do so. I know just what I can do, and I'm going to do it."

"Don't commit yourself to Waddie or his father, Wolf. Either of them would kick you out of your high place as quickly as he put you into it."

"I think everything is going well now, father. The colonel intends to build another boat immediately, and by next spring nobody will trouble the Lake Shore Railroad, except those who live upon the line."

"Don't be too confident."

"I know it! I have been studying up this steamboat business ever since I was discharged by Major Toppleton."

"You are down on the major hard now," said my father.

"No, I'm not. I don't wish him any harm; but while I'm paid for serving the Steamboat Company, I intend to serve it. I've nothing to do with the great men's quarrels; but I'm going to be on time, and do the best thing I can for my employers. I'm going to put her through by daylight."

By this time the steamer was approaching the Horse Shoe Channel, and I went up to the wheel-house. I had taken the bearings so as to pilot the boat through in this direction as well as in the other. By the same process, and with the same precautions, I steered the Ucayga safely through the narrow passage, and we reached the wharf at Ruoara about three minutes inside of the time I had proposed, for the strong wind helped us in going up the lake.

CHAPTER XVI.

TOMMY TOPPLETON MOUNTED.

"ON time!" exclaimed Waddie, as I came out of the wheel-house, after the boat was secured at the wharf.

"Yes, and more too," I replied.   "We are ahead of the Lightning Express this time."

"I want to be reasonable, but I never felt so much like crowing as I do to-day.   By the great horn spoon, I think we have all been asleep on this side of the lake since the Ucayga commenced running," added Waddie, with enthusiasm.

Van Wolter was already moving the freight and baggage on shore; and his zeal had not suffered a particle of diminution.   He worked well, and did not permit a single instant to be wasted.   We had only two trucks, but all the luggage and merchandise they would contain had been piled upon them; and they

11

held nearly all we had to be landed. I wanted two more of these machines, for they could be loaded by the shore men before the arrival of the boat. Then we need stay only long enough to wheel the two trucks on board on shore, and the two on the wharf to the deck. I expected to reduce the delay to three or five minutes.

I stood on the hurricane deck, by the wheel-house, where I could overlook the operations of the mate and the deck hands, and be in readiness to start the boat the instant the last piece of freight was on board. I was delighted with the zeal of the mate, and, I may add, with his politeness and discretion. He did not break things, and he did not tip over the passengers as they came on board. He did not yell like a wild Indian, and say impudent things to gentlemen who incautiously placed themselves in his way. I liked the man, notwithstanding his contempt for me as a boy, manifested at our first meeting. Perhaps I should not blame him for that; but when I had taken the boat through the Horse Shoe Channel, he had done me full justice, and I forgave him. He was my friend, and I was very glad to have done a good thing for him in causing his wages to be raised.

The other steamer would be ready the following spring, and I could not help thinking that Van Wolter would make a first-rate captain for her. At any rate, if he continued to do as well by me as he had thus far, I was determined to speak a good word for him.

"Mr. President, I shall be obliged to ask the company for two more trucks for this landing," I continued, turning to Waddie.

"You shall have a hundred if you want them," replied the little magnate.

"We want only two; and perhaps two more for Ucayga, so that we can get rid of these long delays."

"You shall have everything you want, Wolf. I don't see why we can't beat the Lightning Express every day."

"We can never do it when the train is on time; and I tell you Major Toppleton is too smart to let things drag on the other side as they do just now."

"I don't believe they can go through on time."

"Yes they can. The engineer who is running the dummy now will see that the train is never behind time when they give him the place. I never missed a connection while I was on the road."

"Lewis Holgate is not you."

"But the major will not let him ruin the enterprise much longer."

"Pooh! what can the major do as long as Tom Toppleton chooses to keep Lewis on the engine?"

"Well, Tommy won't choose to keep him there."

"I think he will."

"But Major Toppleton has another string to his bow. Our cake will be dough in a week or so at the most — just as soon as the major fully understands the matter; and I think it won't take him more than a week to see through the millstone."

"You mean to say that he will not let his boats come to Centreport."

"Certainly not. Then you can't get a single through passenger. That is what we are coming to in a short time, unless we find some way to counteract the major's plan."

"Well, can't we find some way?" asked Waddie, anxiously.

"Perhaps we can. I haven't had time to think

of the matter much," I replied, as Van Wolter ordered the men to cast off the fasts and haul in the plank.

I went into the wheel-house, rang the bell, and the Ucayga moved on. I gave the helm to the mate as soon as he came up. Waddie went below to talk with his father, to tell him, I suppose, that our victory was to be but a transient one.

"How's the time, Captain Penniman?" asked the mate.

"Five minutes of five," I replied, consulting my watch, and thinking of Grace Toppleton, as I always did when I saw it, for she had presented it to me in behalf of the Toppletonians.

And I was at variance with them now! No, not with many of them; only with Tommy and a few of his toadies. But I did not like to wear the watch, which had been the gift of those on the other side, for which Major Toppleton had probably paid the lion's share, after the disagreeable events which had occurred. The thought came to me that I ought to return it to the donors; but this was rather a violent alternative for saving my pride.

" We were not more than ten minutes at the Ruoara landing, then," added the mate.

"No; you have done admirably, Mr. Van Wolter, and I thank you for your zeal."

" O, that's all right! I always mean to do my duty while I have any sort of fair play," answered the gratified man.

" We must do our duty whether we have fair play or not," I added. " That's my motto."

" Well, I don't know about that."

" Two wrongs don't make a right. The safest, and indeed the only way for us, is always to do our duty."

" I rather think you are right, after all. We are waxing the Lightning Express over there, this afternoon. That short cut through the Horse Shoe Channel did the business for us."

" That's so; and I've been thinking of it for a long time. I suppose, if I had mentioned it before I did it, I should have been laughed at."

" That's a fact. You have done a big thing to-day, young man; I beg your pardon — Captain Penniman."

" O, we don't stand on any ceremony! We shall be

good friends; and while we stick together, we can accomplish any reasonable thing."

"Didn't I hear you and the colonel saying something about another boat like this one?"

"Yes; the colonel intends to build another — to be called the Hitaca — at once."

"I suppose it is too soon to say anything yet; but I want the command of that boat when she is built," continued Van Wolter, anxiously.

"I was thinking of that very thing myself; and, if you are always as faithful as you have been to-day, I think you will deserve it. I shall mention the matter to the colonel and Waddie as soon as I get a chance."

"Thank you; thank you, captain. That's very handsome of you; and you shall never have any cause to complain of me," he replied, warmly.

"Of course, I can't promise anything; but I will do what I can, if everything is right," I answered.

We discussed the former management of the boat, and I explained to him my plans for the future. We were in perfect accord, and I was glad that I had so soon removed all grounds for jealousy, and all tendencies to pull in the opposite direction, on the part of my subordinate. We were approaching Centreport. The train on the railroad, now ten minutes behind time, was coming into Middleport, on the other side of the lake. At twenty-five minutes past five, we were fast to the wharf. The boat going up the lake had not yet left the pier. To my surprise, I found we had quite a number of up-lake passengers, who had taken the word of our runners that we should be in time for the boat at Centreport. We had kept the promise, but it would not always be safe to make it.

We arrived in season to enable Colonel Wimpleton to send for his carpet-bag, and when the steamer for Hitaca touched the wharf he went on board. He was determined not to lose a day or an hour in laying down the keel of the new steamer, and he was going up the lake to make his contracts for this purpose. The boat started on her trip, and my work for the day was finished. Everybody on board was in remarkably good spirits. For the first time, really, the steamer had beaten the Lightning Express; and we intended to "keep doing it" as long as the achievement was possible. I gave the boat into the keeping of Van Wolter, and went on shore. My father could not leave until he had put the engine in order. As everybody's wages had been raised, there was no danger of a conspiracy against the new order of things.

Not until the excitement of the afternoon's stirring work had subsided did it occur to me that I was engaged to go up the lake on Monday with a party in the Belle. Of course it would be impossible for me to keep my engagement to the letter, though I intended to do so in spirit. The long-desired opportunity of doing something for Tom Walton now presented itself. My friend was a thorough and competent boatman, fully my equal, if not my superior. His mother was poor and in ill health, so that she depended mainly upon him for her support. He was, in my estimation, a splendid fellow; and his devotion to his mother, and his constant self-sacrifice for her sake, won my regard and admiration. I had long desired to give him a situation worthy his abilities and character.

Embarking in the Belle, I crossed the lake. After mooring the boat, I went directly to the house of Tom's mother, and was fortunate enough to find my friend at home. He lived in one of the smallest and meanest dwellings in Middleport. I was determined to do a good thing for him, and I thought, after the boat season was finished, I ought to have influence enough, as the commander of the Ucayga, to procure him a first-rate situation for the winter. He came out of the house, and before I had time to open my business with him, the Toppleton Battalion, which was out for drill, came round the corner, and we suspended our conversation to see the parade.

Major Tommy Toppleton was at the head of the column. He had nearly recovered from his broken leg; but he was not able to walk much yet, and was mounted on a medium-sized pony. The moment he saw me, he halted his battalion, and urged his steed almost upon me.

"You villain, Wolf Penniman!" said he, still urging on his pony, as though he intended to crush me under the iron hoofs of the little charger.

"Shan't I hold your horse for you?" interposed Tom Walton, with his inimitable good-nature, as he seized the bridle-rein of the animal.

"Let him alone!" roared Major Tommy, striking

my friend a sharp blow on the back with the flat of his sword.

I was indignant, and inclined to pull the bantam major from his horse: but I remembered his broken leg, or perhaps I should have done so.

CHAPTER XVII.

TOMMY TOPPLETON THREATENS.

TOM WALTON always had a pleasant way of doing an unpleasant thing. I suppose he thought Tommy Toppleton intended to ride over me, or at least intimidate me by the movements of his high-spirited little charger, and as a friend, he considered it his duty to do something in my defence. This was the reason why he asked if he should not hold the little major's horse.

I had hardly seen Tommy since he had broken his leg; but I had no difficulty in believing that he hated me "with a perfect hatred." He was haughty, tyrannical, and overbearing, even to a greater degree, when incensed, than my new-made friend Waddie Wimpleton. He seemed to think I had no business to live, and move, and have my being, after I had ceased to be serviceable to him. He wanted to crush me, and the demonstration of his pony was only suggestive of what the rider really desired to do.

Tom Walton was a tough fellow, and not at all thin-skinned, in the literal signification of the term. He did not mind the blow which Tommy had given him; but, putting himself on the left of the horseman, and out of the convenient reach of his weapon, he backed the pony out into the middle of the street.

"Let him alone!" shouted the major, struggling to hit, and then to punch, my friend with the sword.

"O certainly! I'll let him alone first-rate," laughed Tom, as he released the steed from his iron grasp.

"You puppy, you!" snapped Tommy, foaming with wrath that a plebeian, like my companion, should venture to take hold of the bridle of his steed. "How dare you touch my horse?"

"Well, I haven't much pluck; but I didn't want him to tread on Wolf's corns."

"Wolf's a rascal, and you're another!"

"Then we are well matched," chuckled Tom Walton.

"If I don't clean you fellows out of this place, it will be because I can't!" snarled Tommy.

"What's the matter, Major Toppleton?" I inquired,

my indignation entirely appeased by the pleasant manner in which my companion had treated the case.

"Wolf, you are a traitor!" exclaimed Tommy, with
emphasis.

"Well?"

"You are an adder, that bites your best friends!"

"I think you are an adder, major, for you are adding
one hard word to another," laughed Tom Walton.

"Don't give me any of your impudence!"

"Certainly not; I leave that to my betters."

"Wolf, I only halted to tell you that Middleport
will soon be too hot to hold you."

"What do you mean by that, Tommy?" I asked,
gently.

"You know what I mean, well enough. You are
a traitor, and are willing to bite the hand that feeds
you."

"I think not."

"What have we done for you? Where did you
get that watch and chain in your pocket?"

"My friends on this side of the lake gave me the
watch and chain."

"Humph! Well, my father paid for it!"

"Then I shall take the liberty to return it to him," I replied. "If you will relieve me of it now, it is at your disposal."

I took the watch from my pocket, detached the chain from my vest, and offered it to him.

"I don't want it. It only shows what a fellow you are. After all we have done for you, Wolf, you go over on the other side, and do all you can to injure us — to injure the Lake Shore Railroad."

"Allow me to call your attention to the fact that you discharged me," I answered, mildly. "I must work for a living, and when the president of the Steamboat Company offers me a situation at three dollars a day, I can't afford to refuse it."

"Can't you!" sneered he. "Allow me to call your attention to the fact that, after all we have done for you, on this side, you got up a row in the car, and broke my leg."

"You got up the row yourself, as you will remember, if you recall the facts. You insisted upon putting two passengers out of the car after they had paid their fare, and while they were behaving themselves in a proper manner."

"You thought you were going to rule the Lake Shore Railroad. You tried to do it; and that was what made the row. Do you suppose I would submit to your dictation? Do you think I had not the right to discharge an employee of the road? I don't see it."

"Probably we shall not make much by discussing the matter here, though, if you wish to do so, I will meet you for that purpose when and where you please," I replied.

"I'll meet you on Monday forenoon, at ten o'clock," said he, suddenly and maliciously.

"I am engaged then. Of course I mean any time when my business will permit."

"I thought you didn't mean what you said," added he, turning up his nose, and pursing out his lips. "I want to give you a fair warning. The Wimpletons wouldn't have you on the other side after you had turned traitor to them. I don't blame them; and we won't have you on this side after you have turned against us. If you mean to stay on this side of the lake, you must have nothing to do with that steamer."

"Don't you think our family has a right to live on this side of the lake?" I inquired.

TOMMY TOPPLETON MOUNTED. Page 170.

"No matter whether you have or not. We won't have you here," replied Tommy, sharply.

"I think we shall stay as long as we think it best to do so. I will return this watch to your father, and then I believe I shall not owe him anything."

"Didn't my father save all the property you had when Wimpleton foreclosed the mortgage?"

"He did; he was very kind to us then, and we shall always gratefully remember all that he did for us, though he was not called upon to pay out a single dollar on our account."

"And for this you are doing your best to ruin the Lake Shore Railroad, which cost my father two hundred thousand dollars! Deny that, if you can!" stormed Tommy.

"I do deny it."

"Are you not running that steamer on the other side?"

"I have that honor."

"Hasn't she beaten the Lightning Express train twice to-day?"

"If she did, it was in fair and honorable competition.

12

You discharged me, and you are responsible for the consequences, not I."

"What's the use of talking to an ingrate, like you!" exclaimed the major, impatiently. "I give you fair warning that I intend to clean you out of the place, the whole kit of you, Tom Walton included."

"All right! It is your next move, Tommy. I hope you won't burn your fingers in the scrape, as you have done several times before."

"Do you threaten me?"

"No, by no means. I only wish to tell you that those who act unjustly must bear the burden of their own injustice. When you attempted to have me put out of the car, it cost you a broken leg, though that was by no act of mine. I shall try to keep the peace, but if attacked, I shall defend myself. For all the good you and your father have done to me and mine, I shall remember you kindly. I shall forgive and forget all the injury. I stood by you and your father as long as you would let me. I refused the very situation which I have now accepted when in your employ, for no money could tempt me to forsake my friends. I hope you will not try to get up a quarrel with me, Tommy, for I have no ill will towards you, and would rather serve you now than injure you."

"Do you mean that?"

"Upon my word I do!" I answered, earnestly; "and if I know my own heart, I spoke the simple truth."

"Perhaps we will give you a chance to prove what you say," said Tommy, with an incredulous shake of the head. "Attention — battalion! Forward — march!"

As abruptly as he had come upon me, he left me. Evidently my words had suggested some plan to him, and I had a right to expect some proposition from him. To sum up Tommy's threats, he intended to drive me out of the town — not by force or by legal measures, but by making "the place too hot to hold me;" which, being interpreted, meant that he and his friends would vex and annoy our family until we should be glad to seek a new home elsewhere. Of course a man so influential as Major Toppleton, senior, had the power to make Middleport very disagreeable to us.

"Tommy's dander is up," said Tom Walton, as the battalion marched up the street.

"It doesn't take much to bring his wrath up to the boiling point," I replied.

"I think you have given them an awful heavy dose to-day, Wolf, if all the stories are true," added Tom, rubbing his hands as though he enjoyed the situation.

"What stories?"

"They say that Colonel Wimpleton, or Waddie, made you captain of the Ucayga."

"That's so."

"And your father the engineer."

"That's so, too."

"Then the boat beat the Lightning Express both ways."

"All true."

"There's a big excitement on this side of the lake. Everybody says Lewis Holgate must step down, and take the dummy."

"I'm willing."

"Can you beat them then, Wolf?"

"We can beat them on the down trip from Centre-port. But we don't expect to do much till next spring; then the Lake Shore Railroad may hang up its fiddle, except for business with Middleport and the towns upon the line."

"Is that so?" asked Tom, opening his eyes.

"No doubt of it. But I wanted to see you about another matter. Have you any work on hand?"

"Nothing but odd jobs," replied Tom, suddenly looking as sad as it was possible for so good-natured a fellow to look. "I must find something to do that will pay me better, or it will go hard with my mother this winter. She isn't able to do much."

"I can put you in the way of doing something for a week or two, which will pay you pretty well. The Belle is engaged to go up the lake next week with a fishing party; but, as things are now, I can't go with her."

"I'm your man!" exclaimed Tom, his eyes sparkling with pleasure, for this was a job after his own heart.

"All right. Let us settle on the terms."

"O, you may fix them to suit yourself."

"How much are you making now, Tom? I don't want to be hard with you."

"You won't be hard with me," laughed he.

"But let us have the matter understood. I will do as well as I can by you. How much do you earn now?"

"Some days I make a quarter of a dollar; some days a half; and I have earned a dollar. If I get three dollars a week I am pretty well satisfied."

"I am to have five dollars a day for the boat when she it taken by the week, and seven for a single day. Suppose I give you two dollars a day for every day the Belle is used."

"That's handsome!" exclaimed Tom. "I shall be rich on those terms."

"No, you won't. She will not have anything to do for more than two or three weeks this season. In the spring she will do well. After she is paid for, we will divide equally."

"Thank you, Wolf. You are a glorious fellow!"

We went down to the Belle's moorings, and I gave my friend such instructions as he needed. I was sure my party would have no reason to regret the change in the skippership of the boat.

CHAPTER XVIII.

THE TWO MAJORS.

TOM wanted to sail the Belle a while, in order to ascertain her points; and though it was now dark, he unmoored her, and stood up the lake. After I had called upon the gentleman who had engaged the Belle, to explain the change in my arrangements, — which, as the person knew Tom very well, were entirely satisfactory, — I went home. My father had just returned from the other side; and I found our family in the most cheerful frame of mind. Our star appeared to be in the ascendant again.

"I have been warned out of town, father," said I, as we sat down to supper.

"Who warned you?" asked my father, with a smile which indicated that he did not consider the warning as of any great consequence.

"Tommy Toppleton. He halted his battalion, and

pitched into me as though he intended to crush me beneath the hoofs of his steed."

I went on to explain what the little major had said; but none of us were alarmed. My mother counselled moderation, as she had always done, and father thought we could make the most by minding our own business.

"I told Tommy I would rather serve him than injure him; and if I know myself, I spoke the truth," I added,

"That's right, Wolfert! I'm glad you said that, for I know you meant it," said my good mother. "While we do our duty, and endeavor to serve the Lord faithfully and patiently, we shall triumph in the end. It does not make much difference if we are cast down for a time, or if wicked men seem to have conquered us; we shall prosper if we are good and true. We can afford to wait for success as long as we do our duty. As the minister said last Sunday, God does not always call that success which passes for such in this world. Real success is in being ever faithful to God and conscience."

I believed what my mother affirmed; but it always

did me good to hear her repeat the lesson of wisdom and piety. It always strengthened my soul, and helped me to maintain my standard of duty. My father was not a religious man, though he always went to church, and had a high respect for sacred things. He always listened in silence to the pious admonitions of my mother; but I was sure he approved them, and believed in them.

Before we rose from the table, the door bell rang, and my mother, who answered the summons, informed me that Major Toppleton desired to see me immediately at his own house.

"What does that mean?" asked my father, manifesting much interest in the event.

"I don't know; but the message reminds me of what Tommy said when we parted," I replied.

"What did he say?"

"When I told him I would rather serve than injure him, he replied that perhaps I might have a chance to prove what I said."

"It may be that the major intends to make you an offer," added my father. "I have no doubt he feels very sore about the events of this afternoon."

"Very likely he does, for we certainly beat the Lightning Express all to pieces; and I am confident we can do it every time we try, on the down trip."

"Suppose he should make you an offer?" inquired my father, anxiously. "What if he should offer you three or four dollars a day to run the Lightning Express?"

"I am glad you asked the question, father, for my mind is made up. I may be wrong, but I think I am right. I should decline the offer."

"If he offered you more wages than the colonel agreed to pay you?"

"Colonel Wimpleton has fairly engaged me to run the Ucayga," I replied, taking my hat from the nail. "It would not be right for me to leave him without giving him reasonable notice of my intention to do so."

"Certainly not. As long as he uses you well, you are bound to do the same by him, whatever happens."

"I refused to leave the railroad company when the colonel offered me more wages than I was receiving. He has given me my place in good faith. If I can do better on this side of the lake than I can on the other, I think I have the right to resign my situation, if I give reasonable notice."

"Quite right, Wolf," replied my father, warmly. "Major Toppleton discharged us both without an hour's notice, and I don't think we are under special obligation to him for his recent treatment of us, though he certainly did us a good turn when we were persecuted by Colonel Wimpleton."

My father and I were in perfect accord, as we generally were on questions of right and of policy; and I hastened to the major's house, not without a certain dread of confronting the great man. I was admitted to the library. I had hoped I should obtain at least a sight of Grace, but I did not; and I braced my nerves for the interview with the great major and the little major, for both of them were present. The father bowed loftily and haughtily as I entered, and the son looked supercilious and contemptuous. Neither of them was courteous enough to invite me to take a seat, and I stood up before them, waiting their imperial pleasure.

"You sent for me, Major Toppleton, and I have

come," I ventured to say; and the cold reception accorded to me had a tendency to make me stand upon my dignity.

"I find, to my surprise, that you have gone into the employ of Colonel Wimpleton," said the senior major, with a sneer upon his lips.

"Yes, sir," I replied, bowing.

"I am astonished!" added the major.

"Neither my father nor myself could afford to remain without employment, when good offers we.e made to us," I answered, respectfully.

"Then I am to understand that you and your fath have arrayed yourselves against me."

"By no means, sir."

"Do you not understand that Wimpleton's steamei and the Lake Shore Railroad are running against each other?" demanded my late patron, severely.

"I do, sir; but I do not think that a fair business competition means any personal ill-will. If it does, it is entirely a matter between you and Colonel Wimpleton. I am not the owner of the Ucayga, and she will run just the same whether I go in her or not."

Major Toppleton bit his lips. Perhaps he felt that my point was well taken.

"You ran the steamer this afternoon, and, by your knowledge of the Horse Shoe Channel, made a quick trip. Those who know say you took the steamer through in fifteen minutes less than her usual time. I hold you responsible, therefore, for this day's work."

" Of course I did the best I could for my employers, as I was in the habit of doing when I ran on the railroad."

" After doing as much as I have for you and your father, I did not expect to see you both arrayed against me."

"But you discharged us both, sir. What could we do ? We could not afford to refuse good offers."

" If the Evil One should offer you a price, would you sell your soul to him ? "

"Decidedly not, sir. It did not happen to be the Evil One who made us the offers, and they were accepted."

" It was the same thing!" exclaimed the major, bitterly.

"Let me talk, father," said Tommy, who, by a miracle which I could not comprehend, had thus far remained silent.

His father let him talk, and, like an obedient parent, was silent himself.

"Wolf, you said you would rather serve me than injure me," continued the little major, fixing his gaze upon me.

"I did; and I meant so," I replied.

"Suppose I should offer to give you back your place on the locomotive."

"It will be time enough to answer when you have done so."

I had no idea that he intended to make me any such offer. The sneers and the looks of contempt bestowed upon me were sufficient assurances that neither father nor son regarded me with any other feeling than aversion. It was not necessary gratuitously to decline the offer in advance, and thus provoke their anger.

"Suppose I should make you the offer," repeated Tommy, rather disturbed by my evasive reply.

"As you have not made it, I need not answer."

"I don't like to make an offer, and then have it refused."

"I do not like to say what I will do till I have an opportunity to do it," I answered.

"You need not bother your head about it. I don't intend to make you an offer. I only wanted to show you that you did not mean what you said about serving me," continued Tommy, spitefully. "I wouldn't — "

"Stop a minute, Tommy," interposed his father. "Wolf, after all we have done for you, we have a right to expect something better of you."

"What would you have me do, sir?" I asked.

"Do! I'll tell you. Go to Wimpleton to-night. Resign your situation. Then come to me, and I'll talk with you about a place for — "

"Stop a minute, father," said Tommy. "Don't make any promises. I wouldn't have him on the Lake Shore Railroad any more than I would have Wimpleton himself. He's a hypocrite — would rather serve me than injure me! Let him resign his place on this steamer! That would be doing something to serve me. After that it will be time enough to talk."

I made no reply, for it was patent to me that Tommy had sent for me merely to bully me. It was easier and cheaper to bear it than to resent it.

"Perhaps you think you can ruin the Lake Shore Railroad, in which I have invested so much money," sneered the senior major.

"I have no desire to do so."

"But you are trying to do it," added Tommy.

"I intend to work for the interests of my employers. If I have an opportunity to serve you, I shall do so, but not by being unfaithful to those who pay me for my work."

"That's just what you did when in my employ," said the father. "You made your peace with Wimpleton in my yacht, feeding him and taking care of him at my expense."

"I did only an act of humanity towards him," I answered, stung by the charge.

"No matter! You are a traitor and a renegade. Go your way, and take the consequences of your treachery. But let me tell you and Wimpleton that when I have made my next move, your steamer might as well be at the bottom of the lake as to attempt to compete with the road."

I bowed, and left, though I did not escape till Tommy had again poured out the vials of his wrath upon me.   If the major had published his "next move" to the world. I could not have understood it any better. The up-lake steamers were no longer to make a landing at Centreport, where the Ucayga could get any of her through passengers.   I went home and told my father the result of the interview.   He only laughed at the impotent rage of the two majors.

Early on Monday morning, as my father and I were pulling across the lake in my old skiff, we saw the Grace — Major Toppleton's yacht — get under way and stand up the lake.   This movement explained what occurred on the arrival of the morning boat from Hitaca.

13

CHAPTER XIX.

THE MAJOR'S NEXT MOVE.

ON Monday morning, at quarter past eight, the Ucayga was in readiness to start as soon as the steamer should arrive from Hitaca. She was in sight, and our runners were on the wharf, prepared to induce through travellers to leave her for our more elegant and spacious boat. Waddie was on board, as excited as though the success of the whole scheme depended entirely upon him.

The up-lake steamer was approaching the Narrows; but, instead of heading directly towards the pier on the Centreport side, as usual, she hugged the west shore. We did not suspect that any change in her movements would be made at present; at least not before it was duly announced in the advertisements and posters of the company. I expected to hear of a different arrangement in a week or two, after Major

Toppleton had thorougly tested the capacity of the railroad and steamers.

"What does this mean, Wolf?" demanded Waddie, blandly, as the Hitaca boat stopped her wheels near the Middleport landing.

"It means that she is not coming to Centreport with her through passengers," I replied, hardly less chagrined than the president of the Steamboat Company.

"But she has no right to do that," protested Waddie, who, like the two great men, had the idea that no one could be justified in acting contrary to his interest and his wishes.

"I suppose the owners of that line have the right to run their boats where they please."

"But they have not advertised any change in their arrangements."

"They are responsible for what they do," I added.

"They must have passengers on board who wish to come to Centreport."

"Probably the boat will come over here after the Ucayga starts. Of course this is a plan on the part of Major Toppleton to prevent us from taking any of his through passengers. We can't expect the Railroad Company, which controls those boats, to play into our hands."

"But we can expect fair play."

"Hardly," I replied.

"But what can we do?" demanded Waddie, intensely nettled by this movement of the other side.

"We can do nothing, just now. I expected this thing, though not quite so soon."

"As the matter stands now, then, we are beaten."

"Just now we are; but I think we shall not stay beaten long," I continued, good-naturedly. "Your father understands the matter perfectly, and has not lost a moment in preparing for the emergency. When we have the other steamer, we shall be on the top of the wave again."

"But must we keep quiet until the other boat is completed?"

"Perhaps not, Waddie, though we cannot fully compete with the other side till we have the new boat. I wonder if your father came down in that steamer."

"I don't know. I think not. He has not had time to do his business in Hitaca."

"I have a plan to propose, and when we have time, I will talk it over with you."

"You always have a plan to propose," said Waddie, beginning to look more hopeful. "Perhaps I will see you when you return, for I must go to school this morning. I haven't forgotten what I said on Saturday."

"I hope not. If I were you, I would not say anything to any one that I had made certain good resolutions. Let them find it out by your actions rather than your promises."

"I will, Wolf; but I am so excited about that steamboat business that I can't think of much else."

"Control yourself, Waddie. Do your duty faithfully at school, and I will try to have everything go right with the boat."

"I am vexed at this change in the running of those boats. It throws us completely out of our plans."

"We must expect such things. We can't have it all our own way, and we must make the best of the circumstances as we find them."

"Major Toppleton is smart."

"I told you he would not be content to have the

wind taken out of his sails. He rose early this morning, and went up the lake in his yacht. Probably he
went on board of that steamer at Gulfport, and directed
her captain to proceed directly to Middleport, instead
of coming to Centreport first."

"What is your plan, Wolf? I am curious to know
about it. Do you mean to start from Middleport?"

"No, we can't do that. Major Toppleton controls
the water front of the town, and we could not get
a landing-place there."

"But don't my father control the water front on
this side? Don't we let the major's boats land
here?"

"Certainly; and it would be very unwise in your
father to prevent them from doing so; for he would
thus shut off from Centreport all direct communication
with Hitaca, and the other towns up the lake. When
he has established a through line, he can afford to
keep his wharves for the exclusive use of his own
boats, though I question the policy of doing so, even
then."

"By the great horn spoon, Wolf, you have a long
head!"

"Thank you, Waddie!"

"But you have not told me about your plan."

"I'm afraid I have not time to do so now," I replied, looking at my watch. "It is nearly half past eight."

"Well, I will see you when you return from Ucayga."

Waddie remained with me till I gave the order to cast off the fasts and haul in the planks. It was evident by this time that the boat from Hitaca was not coming to Centreport until after we had started; and at precisely half past eight, the Ucayga left the wharf. We had quite a respectable number of passengers, though, of course, we had not a single one from up the lake; and, under the new arrangement, we could not possibly have one in the future. It was certainly vexatious, as Waddie had suggested, to be checkmated in this manner, and I knew that Colonel Wimpleton would storm furiously when he heard of it.

I had expected it; and, after the first shock, I felt reconciled to the misfortune. Under the present arrangement, the Ucayga accommodated only Ruoara and Centreport, and till we could offset the movement of Major Toppleton, she must be run only for their benefit.   There was not more than half business enough to support her.   The plan which I had devised, and of which I had spoken to Waddie, had its advantages and its disadvantages; but I was sure that it would be a paying operation for the steamer.   I was very anxious to state it to the colonel and Waddie.

As soon as the Ucayga left the wharf, the Hitaca boat started for Centreport.   The major did not intend to lose any Centreport trade, and by the arrangement he saved his up-lake passengers for that town. Doubtless he was a happy man, and Tommy was satisfied that he had again thrown the magnificent steamer into the shade.   Well, they had, to a certain extent; but it was our next move.

We were at the wharf in Ruoara on time; for the Ucayga, under favorable circumstances, rather exceeded her rate of sixteen miles an hour.   Waddie had sent up the two trucks which I required, and we made our landing in about five minutes.   I took the wheel when the boat left the wharf, and carried her safely through the Horse Shoe Channel; and this time without a particle of the nervousness which had disturbed me before.

I gave Van Wolter the bearings, so that he could be preparing himself for the task, when occasion should require.

But, really, there was now no reason to go through the narrow channel. As we had no possible chance of obtaining any through passengers, it was useless to wait for the up-lake boats, though under my proposed arrangement it would have enabled me to save the day. The mate carefully noted the bearings I pointed out to him, and the operations which I explained. He was a skilful man in his business, and I had no doubt he would soon be a competent pilot for the channel.

While we were going through the passage, the Lightning Express dashed along the other side of the lake; and I was satisfied, from its increased speed and punctuality, that Lewis Holgate had been superseded. The locomotive was evidently under the charge of a skilful hand. But the spirited competition of Saturday, which I had anticipated would continue for a few days, seemed to be at an end. The Ucayga was on time, and so was the train. The passengers from the latter came over on the ferry, and as they landed, I saw Major Toppleton and Tommy. A great crowd of people had come down on the Lightning Express, the larger part of whom were through travellers.

To my surprise, my late patrons walked towards the boat. Both of them looked extremely pleasant, as well they might, after the large freight they brought down, at two dollars a head, from Ithaca. They saw me, as I stood on the hurricane deck, overlooking the landing of our merchandise.

"Good morning, Wolf," said the senior major. "I hope you are very well this morning."

" Quite well, I thank you, sir," I replied, as cheerfully as I could.

Both majors laughed; they could not help it after the victory they had won; and I tried to laugh with them, but it was rather hard work. The father and son came on board, and presently joined me on the upper deck.

"This is a magnificent boat, Wolf," said the great man.

"Yes, sir, she is a very fine boat," I replied.

"I had no idea she was so well fitted up. You did not have many passengers down — did you, Wolf?"

"Not so many as we desired, sir."

"I suppose you remember what I said Saturday night?" chuckled the major.

"Yes, sir."

"I told you it was my next move."

"Yes, sir, I recollect that you said so."

"Well, Wolf, I have made that move."

"I see you have, sir; and, without any disrespect to you, perhaps Colonel Wimpleton will conclude to make the next move himself."

"The next move!" laughed the major. "We think on our side, that we have him in a tight place."

"He don't think so himself, Major Toppleton; and I'm sure I don't."

"What do you mean, Wolf?"

"You seemed to be very much pleased with your success, and I congratulate you upon it. It's all fair."

"Of course it's all fair; but what is your next move?" asked the major, trying to conceal a shade of anxiety that crossed his face.

"As you did not tell me what your move was to be, I think I will keep still for the present, especially as it is not yet matured."

"That's all gas, Wolf," interposed Tommy. "You can't do nothing."

"Perhaps we can't; but we can try," I replied, good-naturedly.

The ferry-boat rang her bell, and my guests departed, though I offered them a passage in the Ucayga.

CHAPTER XX.

GRACE TOPPLETON FAINTS.

IT was certainly our next move, and after the Ucayga left the wharf, I went into my stateroom, abaft the wheel-house, to make some figures relating to my plan. My apartment was a little parlor, and though I had scarcely been into it before, I was very much pleased with it. Besides a berth, in which a nice bed was made up, the state-room was provided with a desk, lockers for books and papers, a couple of arm-chairs, a table, and other suitable furniture.

This was not the traditional " captain's office " to which passengers are invited to step up by the boy with the bell. The office was abaft the port paddle-box on the main deck; and the Ucayga, in anticipation of doing a large business, was provided with a clerk, so that I had nothing to do but attend to the navigation of the boat.

I felt like a lord in my palatial little room, and I was rather sorry that the exigencies of the service did not require me to sleep in it. I sat down at my desk, and was soon absorbed in my calculation. In my own opinion, I had a splendid idea — one which would induce Major Toppleton and his son to call me a traitor again as soon as it was reduced to practice. I had not time to finish writing out the programme before the mate called me, as the Ucayga approached the Horse Shoe Channel.

I took the boat through the difficult passage, and · after we had made the landing at Ruoara, I returned to my room, and finished writing out my plan. Then, with the aid of a handbill which hung up in the apartment, I drew up an advertisement of the proposed new arrangement suitable for the newspapers and for posters, so that, the moment it was approved by Colonel Wimpleton, it could be printed.

I was much excited by the brilliant scheme I had devised, and I was not quite sure that I could not throw the Lake Shore Railroad into the shade, even with one steamer. Certainly with two, the road would be reduced to the condition to which the

major had condemned the Ucayga—that of doing
merely a local business for the towns on its own line.
I was very sorry that Colonel Wimpleton did not return by the morning boat, for I was impatient to show
him my figures, and to have the new programme in-
augurated without any delay.

If the short trips of our boat had done nothing else,
they had hurried up the Lake Shore Railroad; for,
when we reached Centreport, the train had arrived,
and the boat for Hitaca had started. Doubtless Major
Toppleton and his son continued to be perfectly happy,
and believed that they had achieved a decisive and
final victory. For the present they had; but it was
our next move. As I had nearly three hours to spare,
and as Waddie did not appear on board, I went home
for an hour, taking the steamer's jolly-boat, with two
deck hands, to pull me across the lake.

I landed at the steps near the steamboat wharf, and
had hardly ascended to the pier when I had the fortune or the misfortune to confront Tommy Toppleton.
In the enjoyment of his great victory, he had come
down to witness the arrival of the Ucayga, ten or fifteen minutes after the departure of the Hitaca boat.

He looked quite as pleasant as when I had met him down the lake, a couple of hours before.

"How are you again, Wolf?" said he, halting before me on the wharf.

"First rate," I replied. "I hope you are."

"Yes, all but my leg, and that is doing very well. I only limp a little now. You are not on time to-day, Wolf."

"Why, yes; I thought I was. The Ucayga was at her wharf at eleven twenty-five. That was on time, and a little ahead of it."

"But you were not in season for your passengers to go up to Ilitaca in the boat which has just gone."

"No, I was not; but then, you see we had no passengers for Ilitaca. We did not insure any one a connection at Centreport to-day, and so none came by our boat. I did so on Saturday, because your train was ten or fifteen minutes behind time."

"Well, that won't happen again," added Tommy, confidently.

"You haven't fallen out with Lewis Holgate — have you?" I inquired.

"No — O, no! But I persuaded him to go on the dummy, where he is more at home."

"I was satisfied you had some one on the locomotive who understood the business."

"Lewis and I are as good friends as ever."

"I am glad to hear that."

"Are you, Wolf?" sneered Tommy.

"Certainly I am."

I had my doubts whether Lewis Holgate was as good a friend as ever; for, being degraded from the locomotive to the dummy would rankle in his heart, however well he succeeded in concealing his real feelings.

"You haven't resigned your situation as captain of the steamer — have you, Wolf?" asked the little major, with a sinister expression.

"I have not."

"On the whole, I think I wouldn't do it, if I were you," he added, laughing.

"I did not think of doing so, unless the circumstances required such a step."

"Because we are having it all our own way on this side, and we are perfectly willing you should do anything you please now."

"That's handsome; that's magnanimous, Tommy;

14

and I thank you for your condescension," I answered, as cheerfully as I could. "I am very pleasantly situated just now, and it affords me very great pleasure to know that anything in the way of fair competition will not be considered as interfering with your rights and privileges."

"Do anything you like, Wolf. You will be beaten both ways, now, and I think you have come about to the end of your rope. After Colonel Wimpleton has spent so much money on that new steamer, we ought not grudge him the little business he can obtain in Centreport and Ruoara."

"I am glad you feel so, Tommy, and that I have your kind permission to take any step I may think proper."

"Do just what you think best now."

"Thank you."

"I don't mean to say that my opinion of your conduct towards us is at all changed; but as I look at it, your treachery will be its own reward."

"That's rather cool, Tommy. After turning me off with every indignity and mark of contempt you could devise, you talk about my treachery!"

"We won't jaw about that. I don't love you now; but we won't quarrel, if you will only take yourself out of Centreport."

"We may not find it convenient to do that immediately; but probably our business will require us to leave soon."

"We have made our next move, and we are satisfied."

"I hope you won't find any fault when we make ours."

"Certainly not," sneered the little major. "You can't do anything now."

"You may be mistaken; but I hope you will take it as kindly as we do, if things should not go to suit you."

"O, yes!"

"I have your permission to do what I think best," I replied, walking up the pier.

The little major evidently saw no possible way by which the Ucayga could compete with the railroad, as long as the Hitaca boats did not land first at Centreport. I did. I walked to my father's house, thinking over what he had said, and anticipating the storm which would take place when my plan was carried out, as I was confident it would be, as soon as it was submitted to Colonel Wimpleton.

"There has been a gentleman here to see you, Wolfert," said my mother, as I went into the house.

"Who was he?"

"Mr. Portman, or Captain Portman, I think he said. He was very anxious to see you."

"Portman, Portman," I replied, repeating the name, and trying to recall the owner thereof, for it sounded familiar to me.

"He is a stout gentleman, and wore gray clothes."

"O, I know!" I exclaimed, pulling out my pocket-book, and taking therefrom the card of the stout stranger who had pitched Tommy Toppleton out of the car on the railroad.

"He told me, if you came over to-day noon, to send word to him at the hotel."

My mother accordingly sent the message by one of my sisters; and, while she was absent, I related all the events of the forenoon. Presently Captain Portman presented himself. He was very glad to see me, and spoke of me very handsomely, to my face, for my conduct on the railroad.

"As you are no longer in the employ of the Lake Shore Railroad, Wolf, I thought I would like to offer you a place," he said. "But your mother tells me you have a good situation now."

"Yes, sir; I am running the new steamer from Centreport to Ucayga."

"I am sorry you are engaged, though I congratulate you on your splendid situation. I am going to keep a yacht at my place, near Hitaca, and I wanted you to take charge of her next spring, and I will give you plenty of work, and good pay for the winter."

"I am very much obliged to you for your kind offer; but as things stand now, I shall be obliged to decline."

"I see you must; but I am glad to meet you, for I took a fancy to you. My place is only five miles from Hitaca, and I should be pleased to see you there."

We talked for half an hour about affairs on the lake, and I invited him to dine with me; but he was engaged with a friend at the hotel. Just as he was taking his leave, we heard a timid pull at the door-bell.

"Miss Grace Toppleton," said my mother, showing her into the room where we were, which was the parlor.

"Grace!" I exclaimed, delighted to see her.

But I perceived in an instant that she was intensely agitated, and I realized that her visit was not one of ceremony. Indeed, I could not help fearing that some terrible calamity had happened.

"O, Mr. Wolf! I am —"

"Take a chair, Miss Grace," I interposed, as she gasped, and seemed to be entirely out of breath.

I placed the rocking-chair for her, and she began to move towards it. Then I saw that her face had suddenly become deadly pale. Her step tottered, and she was on the point of falling to the floor, when I sprang to her assistance, as did my mother also, at the same time. I received her into my arms, and bore her to the sofa.

"Bless me, the poor child is faint! What can have happened to her?" exclaimed my mother, running for her camphor bottle.

Though it was not very stange that a young lady should faint, I was utterly confounded by the situation. Something had occurred to alarm or agitate her; but I could not imagine what it was. I looked out the window; but I could see no monster, dragon, or ghoul, not even a horse, cow, or dog, to terrify her.

CHAPTER XXI.

GRACE TOPPLETON'S STORY.

MY mother had the reputation of being a skilful person in sickness, or in any emergency. She devoted herself earnestly to the restoration of Grace. I could not help looking at her, alarmed as I was, while she lay pale and beautiful on the sofa. Captain Portman manifested a deep interest in the sufferer, though he knew that she belonged to the family of my persecutor, for the male members of which he had strongly expressed his contempt and disgust.

I tried again to devise some explanation of the singular visit of Grace at our house, and of the violent emotion which agitated her. Although I knew that her father was indulgent to her, I was afraid that everything was not pleasant at home. I had seen her brother strike her a severe blow, and had heard him talk to her in the most violent manner. If he would

GRACE TOPPLETON FAINTS.   Page 214.

behave thus brutally to her in the presence of others, what would he not do in the privacy of his own home? Grace was a true maiden, conscientious, and with the highest views of truth and duty.

It was not difficult to believe, therefore, that some trouble had occurred in the family of the great man of Middleport, and that poor Grace had fled from her home in fear of personal violence. I began to flatter myself, in view of the fact that she had fled to me for protection, and to fancy myself already a first-class knight-errant. I had all along rejoiced in the belief that she regarded me with favor and kindness; but this last act of confidence crowned all my hopes. While I was thinking what I should do for her, how I should shield her from the wrath of her powerful friends, she opened her eyes.

My mother continued her benevolent ministrations until Grace was wholly restored. Probably she was in the habit of fainting; at any rate, she came out of the swoon with a facility which astonished me, and led me to the conclusion that fainting was not the most serious thing in the world, as I had supposed when I saw the fair patient silent and motionless on the sofa. She seemed to gather up her faculties almost as suddenly as she had been deprived of their use.

"Mr. Wolf, I came to see you," said she, after she was able to speak. "I am sorry I fainted; but I have not felt well to-day."

"Rest yourself, Miss Toppleton," interposed my mother. "Don't try to talk much yet."

"I feel much better now, and shall do very well. I am much obliged to you, Mrs. Penniman, for your kindness."

"O, not a bit!" exclaimed my mother.

"But I must do the errand which brought me here, and go home," said Grace, rising from the sofa.

"Don't get up yet, Miss Toppleton; sit still," added my mother, gently compelling her to resume her place on the sofa.

"I feel quite well now. I always faint when anything disturbs me. Mr. Wolf, I have something to say to you."

"Well, I think I will go," said Captain Portman.

"Not yet, if you please, sir," interposed Grace. "What I have to say concerns you also. My father and my brother will be terribly incensed against me if they know that I have been here."

"They shall not know it from any of us," I replied.

"I am sorry that my brother hates you, Mr. Wolf, and sorry that my father indulges all his whims. My mother and I think that they do very wrong; but we can't help it. Just before I came away from home, I heard them talking together about the gentleman who put my brother out of the train at the time his leg was broken. That was you, sir, I believe?"

Captain Portman bowed his acknowledgment of the fact.

"They were talking about arresting you, sir, and taking you before the court for an assault upon Tommy."

The stout gentleman smiled, as though it were not a very serious matter.

"But I don't think I should have come here if this had been all," continued Grace. "My brother saw and recognized you in the street, sir."

"Very likely," nodded Captain Portman.

"Dear me, I must hurry on with my story, or I shall be too late to do any good!" exclaimed the fair visitor. "Well, my brother is determined that you shall be arrested, too, Mr. Wolf. He insists that you were concerned in the assault. They have gone to find an officer now. Tommy says he shall prevent your running that steamboat this afternoon, and perhaps for a week; and this is really what my brother wants to do, so far as you are concerned, Mr. Wolf."

Was this all? And Miss Grace had not been driven from her home by the persecution of her father and brother! Tommy had not even struck her again! I was really glad, when I came to think of it, that the matter was no worse. If I had no opportunity to do desperate deeds in the service of my beautiful friend, I had the consolation of knowing that there was no occasion for any. I was happy to realize that peace reigned in the great mansion.

When my anxiety for Grace would permit me to think of myself, I appreciated the obligation under which she had placed me by this timely warning. I was willing to be arrested for my agency in expelling Tommy from the train, for, being entirely innocent, I could afford to face my accusers.

"Now, what will you do, Mr. Wolf?" asked Grace, beginning to be much agitated again.

"First, I shall be under everlasting obligations to you for your kindness in taking all this trouble on my account."

"Never mind that, Mr. Wolf," she said, blushing. "I know you had nothing to do with injuring my brother, and I do not want you to suffer for this, or to have your steamboat stopped for nothing. The constable and Tommy are going to wait for you at the corner of the street," she added, indicating the place where I was to be captured. "You must go some other way."

"I will, Miss Grace."

"And I will go and throw myself into the hands of the Philistines at once," added Captain Portman, laughing.

"I suppose they can't hurt you, sir," said Grace.

"Well, I am certainly guilty of the offence charged upon me," replied Captain Portman. "I will not now pretend to justify it, though your brother was very unreasonable, and detained me, as well as a crowd of others, without the slightest excuse for doing so. The act was done in the anger and excitement of the moment, and I shall cheerfully submit to the penalty of the law, as a good citizen should do."

I thanked Miss Grace again for her interest in me, and for the trouble she had taken on my account. What she had done was no trivial thing to her, as her fainting fully proved, and I could not but be proud of the devotion she had exhibited in my cause. She took her leave; and after she had been gone a few minutes, Captain Portman departed.

Tommy's plan included me in the arrest for an assault upon him; but that was only a conspiracy to injure the steamboat line on the other side of the lake. I deemed it my duty to defeat this little scheme, in the interests of my employers. I ate my dinner hastily, and then left the house by the back door, making my way to the lake, where I had left my skiff, by a round-about course. I pulled across, and as I went on board of the Ucayga, I hoped the constable who was waiting for me would have a good time.

I was not quite sure that Grace had not made a mistake, so far as I was to be connected with the arrest. She might have misunderstood the conversation she had heard; for I could hardly believe it possible that Major Toppleton intended to have me arrested. Everybody knew that I had had no hand in putting Tommy out of the car.   No one had ever asserted such a thing.   But they could affirm that I was in company with Captain Portman at the time, and that I had instigated him to do the deed.   Of course this was nonsense; but it might be a sufficient pretence to detain me long enough for the Ucayga to lose her afternoon trip.   The warning I had received induced me to prepare for the future, and I instructed the mate to run the boat through, if at any time I should be absent when it was time to start.

I went into the engine-room, and told my father what had transpired during my absence.   He listened to me, and seemed to be much annoyed by my story; for it looked like the first of the petty trials to which we were to be subjected, in accordance with Tommy's threats.   While I was thus employed, Waddie Wimpleton appeared, excited and anxious under the defeat we had that day sustained.

"I am sorry your father did not come down this morning," said I, after he had expressed his dissatisfaction at the movement of Major Toppleton.

"Why?" asked Waddie, hopefully.

"Because I have a plan to propose to him."

" Can't you propose it to me?" said he, laughing. "I am the president of the Steamboat Company."

" I know you are; but I did not think you would be willing to take a step so decided as the one I shall propose, without the advice and consent of your father."

"Let me hear what it is, and then I can tell you whether I will or not."

" Come to my state-room, then, and I will show you all the figures. If I mistake not, we can do a big thing, even before the keel of the Hitaca is laid down."

" I have been thinking a good deal about our affairs to-day, Wolf," said Waddie, as we went upon the hurricane deck. " I have tried to feel kindly towards the folks on the other side. It's hard work, and I'm not up to it yet — by the great horn spoon I'm not!"

" You must not try to overdo the matter," I replied, pleased with his enthusiasm.

" They are endeavoring to injure us all they can. If Major Toppleton had not prevented his boat from coming to Centreport this morning, it would have been easier to feel right towards him."

" You need not feel unkindly towards him on that

account. Major Toppleton, as an individual, is one affair; his railroad and steamboat line is quite another. A fair competition is all right. We will not say a word, or do a thing, against the major or his son, personally; but we must do the best we can for the success of our line. We are in duty bound to do it, as much for the public good as our own. If we lessen the time between Hitaca and Ucayga by an hour, so far we confer a benefit upon the travelling community. We need have no ill will towards any person. If the major and his son need our help, our kind words, let them be given. We will not say anything to injure their line; but we will do the best we can to build up our own."

"But we don't shorten the time between Hitaca and Ucayga by an hour, or even a minute," said Waddie.

"Perhaps we shall. Sit down, and I will show you the figures," I replied, as I took my programme from the desk.

15

CHAPTER XXII.

OUR NEXT MOVE.

I HAD written out a plan for the running of the Ucayga an entire day. I had studied it out very carefully, and made all the allowances I deemed necessary. The basis of our anticipated success was the fact that our boat would make sixteen miles an hour, while the old steamers were good for only ten, or when crowded, for twelve, at the most. Waddie looked at my time table; but he did not exhibit any enthusiasm, and I concluded that he did not understand it.

"What do you think of it?" I inquired, somewhat amused by the puzzled expression on his face.

"I dare say it is first rate; but I don't exactly know what all these figures mean. I see Hitaca on the paper, but of course you don't mean to go up there."

"That's just what I mean," I replied.

"Go to Hitaca!" exclaimed Waddie.

"Certainly — go to Hitaca."

"But my father promised the people of Centreport and Ruoara that they should have two boats a day to Ucayga, and if you go up to the head of the lake, you can't possibly make two trips a day from there."

"That's very true; nevertheless, we will go to Hitaca once every day, and still make the two trips, as your father promised."

"Don't understand it," answered Waddie, hitching about in his chair.

"I'll tell you about it. We are in Centreport now."

"That's so; and I am willing to make oath of that," laughed the president of the Steamboat Company.

"Good! We will begin here, then," I added, pointing to the name of the place on my time table. "We leave here at two-thirty, and arrive at Ucayga so as to start from there at four."

"Just so; that is the programme now."

"We follow the present arrangement in all respects, but with a little addition. We reach Centreport at five twenty-five this afternoon."

"I understand all that," said Waddie, rather impatiently.

"From that point we strike out a new track. Instead of remaining at Centreport over night, we continue right on to Hitaca, stopping on the way at Gulfport, Priam, Port Gunga, and Southport. We shall be Hitaca at seven-thirty, about an hour ahead of the railroad line."

"That will give us a share of the through passengers," added Waddie, as he began to comprehend the nature of my plan. "But I don't see how —"

"Hold on a minute, Mr. President," I interposed. "You agree that my method is all right so far?"

"Certainly."

"We beat the other line on the through run by about an hour."

"That's true."

"Then we shall take all, or nearly all, the through passengers on the afternoon trip up; for none of them will want to waste an hour on the passage. Besides, we give them a perfect palace of a boat, compared with the old steamers."

"O, we shall take them all!" exclaimed Waddie. "There will be no changing, while the railroad line must change twice."

"Still further," I continued. "There is a train for the south which leaves Hitaca at eight in the evening. The old boats are always too late for it; we shall be in season.   That will help us again, for passengers going beyond Hitaca will not have to remain there ever night."

"We shall have it all our own way," said Waddie, rubbing his hands with delight.

"More yet; we can have supper on board, and that will be another source of profit to the boat, and be an accommodation to the passengers, who in the old line have their supper at nine o'clock, after they get to the hotel."

"It's all plain enough so far.   You will stay in Hitaca over night?"

"Certainly; and now for the rest of the plan," I continued, glancing at my programme. "The old-line boat leaves Hitaca at quarter of six in the morning, so early as to be a very great annoyance to passengers. We will leave at half past six — three quarters of an hour later.   We can have breakfast on board, which the old boats cannot for the want of the facilities.   We shall touch at all the intermediate ports, and arrive at

Centreport by half past eight, or so as to leave at our · usual time."

"That's first rate!" exclaimed Waddie. "You get this extra trip to Hitaca by running up at night and down in the morning."

"Exactly so; but we can make only one through trip a day to Hitaca. We shall reach Ucayga at ten in the forenoon, as we do now, and come right back on the return trip. We go from the head to the foot of the lake in three hours and a half, including stops. The railroad line does the same thing in four and a quarter."

"They beat us a quarter of an hour between Centreport and Ucayga, and we beat them an hour between Centreport and Hitaca, making a balance of three quarters of an hour in our favor."

"That tells the whole story, Waddie," I replied.

"But how about the other trip?" asked the president, anxiously.

"Until the Hitaca is built, we must submit to be beaten on that. We can't go up to the head of the lake twice a day with one boat. We leave Ucayga at ten, but we come only to Centreport. In other words, we shall make one trip a day to Hitaca, and two to Centreport, from the foot of the lake."

"That's a good deal."

"So it is; and, by this new arrangement, we shall all have to work from about five o'clock in the morning till eight or nine in the evening."

"That will be rough on you."

"But we shall have to do it only till the other steamer is built. The boat will make a good deal of money. The old line charges two dollars a passenger for through tickets. We can afford to carry them for a dollar and a half."

"But what shall be done about it? This is all talk."

"If your father were here, I think he would send the boat to Hitaca this very night," I replied.

"Then I will do so," added the president, promptly.

"If there is any blame, I will share it with you."

"Go ahead, Wolf! If you only beat the other line, my father will be satisfied. I shall go up to Hitaca with you."

"I will have a state-room ready for you, if you wish to sleep on board."

"Thank you, Wolf."

"But we want some handbills, Mr. President, to inform the public of the new arrangement. You can have them printed so that we can take them as we return, and have them ready to scatter all over Hitaca when we get there to-night."

"I will have them done."

I sat down at my desk, and wrote the following advertisement : —

NO MONOPOLY!

THROUGH LINE TO UCAYGA!

THE NEW AND SPLENDID STEAMER

UCAYGA,

CAPTAIN WOLFERT PENNIMAN,

Will leave Hitaca every day at 6½ o'clock A. M. Touching at Southport, Port Gunga, Priam, Centreport, and Ruoara, and arriving at Ucayga in season to connect with trains East and West. Will leave Ucayga at 4 o'clock P. M., and arrive at Hitaca at 7½ o'clock P. M. Fare, $1.50.

W. WIMPLETON, *President.*

Waddie took this copy, and hastened to the printing office with it. I was confident that this programme

would carry consternation into the ranks of the old
line. After Waddie had gone, I went down to see
my father. I explained my plan to him, and told him
that the boat would go through to Hitaca that night.
He was a prudent man, and suggested some difficul-
ties, nearly all of which I had considered and provided
for. Except at Middleport, the wharves were free to
any one who chose to use them, so that there was no
trouble about the landings. Van Wolter was a pilot
for the upper part of the lake. As the public generally were to be benefited by the new line, we had no
opposition to dread except from the Railroad Company.

At half past two, the Ucayga left her wharf, and, as
usual, arrived at the foot of the lake just before four
o'clock. I had fully explained my purpose to the mate,
and to all on board, that they might make their arrangements to be absent over night. The railroad passengers were already in waiting when we reached
Ucayga, and the trains from the east and west were in
sight. Our runners were duly instructed to "ring in"
for through passengers, at a dollar and a half each, with
the time nearly an hour less than by the railroad line.

This was really the first day of the exciting competition. We had not yet unmasked our great battery, and the victory was still with the Lake Shore Railroad. I was not at all surprised to see Major Toppleton and Tommy among the passengers, as we landed. They had come up a second time that day to enjoy their triumph, and perhaps, also, to look out for the interests of their road. They were quite as pleasant as they had been in the morning, and both of them took the trouble to pay me another visit.

"Well, Wolf, how goes it with the new and splendid steamer?" asked the magnate of Middleport.

"First rate, sir."

"You don't seem to have any through passengers," laughed he.

"No, sir; none on this trip."

"That is very unfortunate for the new and splendid steamer," he added, chuckling.

"Yes, sir, it is rather bad; but we have to make the best of it. We hope to do better by and by."

"I hope you will, for you seem to have plenty of room to spare."

"Yes, sir; rather more than we wish we had."

"I shall be obliged to have some new cars built, for we had about two hundred through passengers by this trip, and we could not seat them all in three cars."

"I wouldn't have any built just yet, Major Toppleton," I answered, pleasantly.

"There will be more passengers before there are less. On our morning trip down, and our afternoon trip up, we are always crowded," chuckled the major.

"If you have more than you can accommodate comfortably, we should be glad to take some of them."

"I dare say you would, Wolf; but the fact of it is, you are so slow that people will not ride with you."

"No use, Wolf," interposed Tommy. "You might as well hang up your fiddle. You can't compete with the Lake Shore Railroad."

"We never say die. We intend to have our share of the business."

"Perhaps you do; but you won't have it," said Tommy, as the two trains came in, nearly at the same time.

"Steamer Ucayga; new boat! Through to Hitaca!" shouted our runners. "No change from boat to cars! Magnificent steamer! Land you in Hitaca at half past seven, gentlemen! Fare only a dollar and a half!"

Major Toppleton and Tommy looked aghast, and turned to me for an explanation.

CHAPTER XXIII.

UP THE LAKE.

"WHAT do you mean, Wolf?" demanded Tommy Toppleton, turning fiercely towards me. "Have you told your runners to lie to passengers?"

"Certainly not," I replied. "They are telling only the truth as I understand it."

"The truth! Don't you hear them?" angrily interposed Major Toppleton.

"I hear them, sir. They are saying just what they have been told to say. You will notice that they do not utter a word against the railroad line."

"But they say your boat is going through to Hitaca!" exclaimed the major.

"So she is, sir."

"To Hitaca!"

"Yes, sir; I mean so."

"Do I understand you that this boat is to run through to Hitaca?" demanded the great man, fiercely.

"That is precisely what my words mean," I replied, calmly. "You will remember that you made your last move this morning. The president of the Steamboat Company makes his last move this afternoon."

"But this is absurd, and impossible. You don't mean it. It is intended to cheat passengers," fumed the magnate.

"All who go with us will be landed at Hitaca at half past seven this evening, if no accident happens."

"But this boat was built to run from Centreport to Ucayga."

"That is very true, sir; but your move this morning compelled the president to change his plans."

"You can't carry them out; and it is an imposition upon the public."

"All that we promise we shall perform."

"But it is simply impossible."

"I think not."

"Do you mean to tell me, Wolf, that this boat can make two trips a day between Hitaca and Ucayga?"

"No, sir, I do not; we only propose to make one through trip a day, with an additional one to Centreport. On our ten-o'clock trip up we shall go only to Centreport."

"This is villanous!" said Major Toppleton, grinding his teeth with rage.

"One of your mean tricks, Wolf!" added Tommy, savagely.

"Really you must excuse me, Tommy, but it was only this morning that I had your kind permission to take any step I thought proper. Didn't you mean so?" I replied.

"You are going to run an opposition line to Hitaca, then?" growled the father.

"And do all you can to injure those who have been your best friends," howled Tommy.

"Why, I was told this forenoon to do what I pleased. This is fair competition. If people wish to ride on the railroad, they may do so. We will not prevent them from going whichever way they please. If you are not satisfied with your last move, you can make another. I am sorry you exhibit so much feeling about the matter," I continued.

"Wolf, this is rascally," said the major, as he saw the passengers crowding on board of the Ucayga. "You have cut under in the price, too."

"The president of the Steamboat Company thinks he can carry passengers for a dollar and a half."

"But I will carry them for a dollar!" exclaimed the major.

"For half a dollar!" added Tommy.

"I do not fix the prices for the Steamboat Company; but I suppose they can carry passengers as cheaply as any other line."

"All aboard for Hitaca!" shouted the runners.

"Gentlemen, this is an imposition!" shouted Major Toppleton, beside himself with rage. "This boat goes only to Centreport!"

"Gentlemen, you shall be landed at Hitaca at half past seven!" I cried, to counteract the effect of his words.

"Passengers by the railroad for Hitaca — fare only one dollar," added the major.

"We'll try this boat once," said a gentleman in the crowd.

By this time the trains were moving off, and the

travellers had chosen by which route they would go up the lake. I ran up the ladder to the wheel-house.

"All aboard, and all ashore!" screamed Van Wolter, as I gave him the word.

The planks were hauled in while the major and his runners were vainly striving to influence the passengers to leave the boat. We had them, and we kept them. Most of them were attracted by the pleasant aspect of the Ucayga, and desired to see more of her. Many had doubtless heard of her, and were anxious to give her a trial. We backed out from the wharf, and were soon on our way up the lake. The people on board were not a little disturbed by the insinuations of Major Toppleton; for, coming from him, they seemed to mean more than if uttered by the runners. I assured them that we should perform to the letter all we had promised. I explained the new plan to some of the regular travellers, and the advantages of the new line were so obvious, that many of them volunteered to patronize the line in future. We were on time, and when the Ucayga arrived at Centreport, the old boat had been gone about ten minutes. We saw her less than two miles distant. Judging from the

16

number of passengers on board of the ferry boat, she had a very small freight. Our case would argue itself with the travelling public, for no one could be so stupid as to prefer the old line, with a change from boat to cars, and from cars to boat again, and requiring three quarters of an hour longer time to make the passage.

At Centreport Waddie appeared with a thousand small handbills, for which I had provided the copy. He brought his valise with him, and I saw that he intended to be a passenger. He was of course very anxious to see the working of the new arrangement. Van Wolter hurried the freight ashore, and in five minutes we were ready to continue our voyage. We were now just fifteen minutes behind the old boat, which we were to beat by forty-five minutes during the trip.

Waddie had taken pains to circulate the information that the Ucayga would go up the lake to Hitaca at half past five, and our crowd of passengers was considerably increased by those who had chosen to wait. The number on board was entirely satisfactory, and her present trip would be a profitable one to her owner. Waddie rubbed his hands with delight when he saw how successful we had been in obtaining through passengers, even before the new arrangement had been advertised; but the steamer was so very attractive in her appearance that travellers could not hesitate long in choosing her.

"You have a big crowd on board, Wolf," said Waddie, after the boat started.

"We have been remarkably fortunate," I replied.

"You have done a big thing for us, captain; and the best thing I ever did was to make peace with you."

"Because you are likely to make money by it!"

"Not that alone. I want to tell you, Wolf, that I have kept my promise so far."

"I am very glad to hear it, and I hope you will persevere."

"I am rather sorry this sharp competition between the old and the new line comes in just now," he added, musing.

"Why so?"

"Because it is only increasing the ill feeling between the two sides of the lake."

"It will afford you the better opportunity to be just, if not generous. The competition on our part shall be fair and honorable."

"But we have cut under in price half a dollar on a trip," suggested Waddie.

"Two dollars is too much for a journey of forty-five miles. The railroad line had a monopoly of the through passengers, and charged what its officers pleased. One dollar and half is a fair price. We will stick to that, if you and your father consent."

"Suppose the major puts the price down to a dollar, or even less?"

"He did that, at Ucayga, this afternoon. He offered to carry all who would go with him for a dollar. I don't think many people will be willing to start three quarters of an hour sooner in the morning, change twice in a trip, and go in those old boats for the sake of saving half a dollar. However, that is to be proved. But a hundred passengers, at a dollar and a half, pay as well as a hundred and fifty at a dollar."

"By the great horn spoon, won't my father be astonished when he sees the Ucayga putting in at Hitaca!"

"No doubt of it."

"He will approve what I have done, I know," added Waddie. "Do you suppose Major Toppleton has gone up in the steamer ahead of us?"

"Probably he has; he will be too anxious to see the working of the new arrangement to stay at home."

"I have been thinking of some way to make peace between our two families," added Waddie.

"Have you, indeed? Well, that is hopeful," I replied.

"I am afraid this rivalry will prevent any coming together, even if my father were willing to make up. Do you feel quite sure that we are doing right in running opposition to the other line?" asked Waddie, seriously; and I could not help thinking of the proverbial zeal of new converts.

"Let us look at it a moment," I answered, willing to take a fair view of the whole subject. "Before the railroad was built, the boats charged a dollar and a half from Hitaca to Ucayga, and went through without any change. Then a Centreport passenger had to cross the lake, go twenty miles by railroad, and then cross back again. Half a dollar was added to the price of passage from one end of the lake to the other. Centreport was not accommodated, and was overcharged. Is there any moral law which compels people to submit to imposition? On the contrary, ought they not to resist? The Steamboat Company carries passengers quicker, more comfortably, and at a less price. It is, therefore, doing the public a service, though at the expense of the other line. Your course is not only right, but commendable. All the people and all the towns on the lake must not suffer in order to make the Lake Shore Railroad profitable to its owner."

"I suppose you are right; but I wish the competition did not add to the ill will between the two sides."

Waddie appeared to be sincere; but it was visionary in him to think of such a thing as reconciling the two houses of Wimpleton and Toppleton, though, of course, such an event was not impossible.

The Ucayga was approaching Gulfport. The old boat had just made her landing there; indeed, she started just in season to allow us to use the wharf. I was rather afraid the bad blood of the major would induce him to throw some obstacle in our way, but nothing of the kind was attempted here. We landed our passengers; but the other boat had taken all who were going up the lake, which she was not to be allowed to do at the other ports.

CHAPTER XXIV.

A TRICK OF THE ENEMY.

THE next port was Priam, eight miles distant; and the Ucayga dashed merrily on' her way, seeming to feel and rejoice in the responsibility which was imposed upon her. Certainly she was doing all that was expected of her. We were approaching the Ruoara; for that was the name of the old boat, though it was a misnomer now to her, for she did not deign to visit the town after which she was called. She was making her best time, which, however, was very poor time, compared with the new boat. Her captain was evidently hurrying her all he could. I made the signal with the steam-whistle, to indicate that the Ucayga intended to pass her on the port hand.

I was not a little startled to see her put her helm to starboard, and crowd over upon our track, as though she intended to bother us. I took the wheel with Van

Wolter, and when she had forced herself in ahead of us, I sounded the whistle to go on the starboard hand of her.

"Give her a wide berth," said I to my companion.

"I reckon we can hit as hard as she can," chuckled the mate.

"But we won't hit at all, either hard or soft," I added.

"She has put her helm to port, as though she did not mean to let us pass her."

"She can't help herself," I answered, as I crowded the helm over, so as to give her a wide berth.

By this time we were abreast of her, and the old tub was so clumsy that she found it impossible to crowd us any further. She had come up so that we could recognize faces on board of her. Near the wheel-house stood the major and Tommy, looking as ugly as they conveniently could look. They would have sunk us in the deep waters of the lake if they could. I was not disposed to irritate them; for I knew how miserably they felt, as they gazed upon our crowded decks, and as they saw our palatial craft sweeping swiftly by them. It did not appear that the Ruoara had more than forty or fifty passengers.

"We can afford to be polite," said I to Waddie. "We will give them the compliments of the day as we pass."

"Don't vex them," replied Waddie.

"If they wish to take a common civility as an insult, they may. On deck, there!" I cried to the hands forward. "Stand by, and dip the ensign and the jack!"

Two of the crew promptly obeyed my order. The ensign at the stern, and the jack at the bow, were dipped three times, just as we came abreast of the Ruoara. Our passengers were disposed to be exceedingly good-natured, and before I was aware of their purpose, they were engaged in giving three cheers, and in demonstrating with hats, handkerchiefs, and other articles. Not a sign of acknowledgment was made by the old boat, and I am afraid that the magnate of Middleport did not feel as happy as the people in our boat. We passed her, and soon left her far behind.

We made our landings at the other ports of the lake, creating no little excitement by our unexpected appearance. We took all the passengers and freight that were waiting for a passage, leaving nothing for the old boat, for the first comer always carried off the prize. Promptly on the time I had marked down on my programme, the Ucayga entered the narrow river on which Hitaca is located. We whistled with tremendous vigor to inform the people of the place of our arrival, for I was very anxious that Colonel Wimpleton should be apprised of our approach.

Van Wolter was perfectly at home in the navigation of this river, and piloted the boat, without any delay, to the broad lagoon which forms the harbor of the town. It was just half past seven when the bow line was thrown on shore, and in a few moments more the steamer was fast to the wharf. Our approach had been heralded through the town, and the landing-place was crowded with omnibuses and other vehicles, which had come down to convey our passengers to the hotels, or to their homes. With them had come a goodly delegation of the solid men of Hitaca, as well as the miscellaneous rabble which always waits upon the advent of any new sensation.

Almost the first person I recognized on the wharf, from my position on the hurricane deck, was Colonel Wimpleton. The Ucayga had been discovered and identified when miles down the lake, and her owner would have learned of her coming, even if he had not been engaged with the steamboat builder on the creek near the wharf. I looked at him with interest, for though we had achieved a triumphant success, we had acted without his sanction, and even without his knowledge.

The moment the boat touched the wharf, the colonel rushed on board, and hastened up to the place where he had seen Waddie and me. He looked as though he was laboring under some excitement, but I had yet to learn whether he was angry or not. Certainly he did not look very gentle; but then his astonishment at seeing the Ucayga at Hitaca was a sufficient explanation of his troubled aspect.

"What does all this mean, Wolf?" he demanded, rather sharply; but this was his habit.

"If any one is to blame, I am the one, for I told Wolf to run the boat to this place to-day," interposed Waddie.

"But what are you here for?"

"We were compelled to come, sir," I replied. "The action of the railroad line left us no other course. If you will walk into my room, sir, I will explain the whole matter; and I hope it will prove satisfactory to you."

"But this is a very strange movement on your part; and without a word from me," said Colonel Wimpleton, as I led the way into my state-room. "You have broken up your trips to Centreport, and there will be a howl of indignation there when I return."

"Not at all, sir. We shall run every trip from Centreport to Ucayga, as usual."

"Well, explain yourself," continued the magnate, impatiently. "Does the boat need repairs, that you have brought her up here?"

"No, sir; she is in good order in every respect. This morning, Major Toppleton made his next move, and we have not had a single through passenger on the down trips to-day. As I supposed he would do, he ordered his boat not to go to Centreport until after our steamer had started. He took his yacht and went over to Gulfport early this morning, so that the first boat did not touch on our side of the lake till the Ucayga had sailed."

"That's one of his tricks."

" Well, sir, I don't know that I blame him. He means business, and he meant to keep all the through passengers. At Ucayga, to-day, he and Tommy crowed over me, and defied me to do anything I pleased. Now, sir, if you look at my time table, you will see that we can, by hard work, make two trips a day from Centreport, and one from Hitaca, to and from the foot of the lake."

The great man put on his spectacles, and proceeded to examine the programme which I had placed in his hands. With the explanations I made, he comprehended the whole subject. His countenance lighted up with pleasure as he realized that he had the means in his hands, even now, to win the day in the battle with his great enemy.

" Why didn't you mention this thing before, Wolf?" he asked.

" I didn't think of it, sir. When Major Toppleton made his next move, as he called it, I went to work on the problem, to see what could be done. I didn't like the idea of running from Centreport with only half a freight. I want to make the boat pay."

" She will pay handsomely under this arrangement. Do you think we need another boat, now?"

"Yes, sir; I do. This boat will be going from half past six in the morning till half past seven at night; and the hands will be on duty from five in the morning till nine at night. The boats will all need repairs, and there will be no time to make them."

"You can have two sets of hands, if you like."

"But we can make only one trip a day from Hitaca to Ucayga."

"Well, that is really enough, for the railroad line has very few passengers up in the morning, or down in the afternoon. We shall take the lion's share of them. This boat-builder has raised his price so much that I have not yet made a contract with him."

"We can try our plan for a while, if you approve it, sir," I replied.

"Certainly I approve it."

Waddie produced the handbills he had procured at Centreport, and a person was employed to distribute them all over Hitaca. Colonel Wimpleton inserted advertisements in the papers, paying liberally for "editorial puffs" of the new line. Everything promised an entire success for the enterprise.

At quarter past eight, the old Ruoara made her

appearance, and moored at the wharf just above the Ucayga. It was a meagre show of passengers which landed from her, and I could well understand the rage which filled the bosom of the major and his son, as they stood upon the hurricane deck gazing at the new steamer. I wondered what their next move would be, for it was not in the nature of either of them to submit to the mortifying defeat they had sustained. I could think of nothing that it was possible for them to do to retrieve their misfortune, unless the major built new steamers, or continued the Lake Shore Railroad to Hitaca.

As they did not come near me, I did not devote much attention to a consideration of their case. Having nothing more to do on board, I took a walk on shore with Waddie. I visited a clothing store, and purchased a suit of blue clothes, which included a frock coat. When I got up the next morning, I put on the new garments, and surveyed myself in the glass. The effect was decidedly satisfactory. I had a glazed cap, for I was not quite ready to don a stove-pipe hat. As I surveyed myself, I had hopes that I should not again be accused of being a boy.

At quarter of six the Ruoara left the wharf. I could not see more than a dozen passengers on board. I looked in vain for Tommy and his father. Soon after, the people began to pour in upon the decks of the Ucayga, to the great satisfaction of Colonel Wimpleton. Our handbills had accomplished their purpose, and our triumph was to be even greater than that of the day before. I was very much excited by the lively scene around me. Carriages, omnibuses, and other vehicles, were constantly arriving with freight and passengers, and I found enough to do in answering questions and hurrying up the men engaged in loading freight. Five minutes before the hour of starting, the scene became a little more quiet. I stood upon the wharf, looking at the situation, when I saw Major Toppleton and his son, accompanied by a stranger, approaching me.

"There he is!" said Tommy, pointing to me with his finger. "Grab him!"

Hearing the words, I deemed it prudent to hasten on board, for I concluded that this was the sequel to the affair of the day before in Middleport. I hurried

17

to the plank; but before I could reach the deck, the stranger seized me by the collar.   I struggled to escape, but the man was too strong for me.

"I have a warrant for your arrest," said he,

A trick of the enemy!

CHAPTER XXV.

THE STEAMBOAT EXCURSION.

"HOLD on to him!" shouted Tommy. "This is our next move."

"I am sorry to trouble you, Captain Penniman; but I must do my duty," said the constable.

"I should like to inquire what all this means," I added, as the officer, finding I did not attempt to annihilate him, let go his hold of me.

"I don't know; the warrant comes up from Middleport. I suppose it is all right."

"Don't stop here with him," interposed Major Toppleton. "Take him away to jail, or some other safe place."

By this time Colonel Wimpleton was at my side with Waddie, both of them so indignant that I was afraid that a scene would transpire on the spot. My powerful patron desired to see the warrant, and the constable, to the great disgust of the major, exhibited the document.

"All right," said Colonel Wimpleton. "This warrant commands you to bring your prisoner before a magistrate at Middleport. Step right on board of our boat, and we will see that you are enabled to obey the command to the letter."

"I am satisfied," answered the constable.

"But I am not," interposed Major Toppleton, angrily.

"All aboard!" shouted Van Wolter.

"I shall do my duty as I understand it," continued the constable, as I led the way to the deck of the Ucayga.

"It is your duty to commit him to jail," growled the magnate of Middleport.

"I will be responsible for the consequences," added Colonel Wimpleton, who could afford to be good-natured, as he saw his great rival defeated in his purpose.

To my surprise, both Major Toppleton and his son followed us on board, and did not offer to go on shore when the plank was hauled in, and the fasts cast off

They had evidently remained at Hitaca for the purpose of carrying out the little scheme they had contrived; and, having done their worst, they had no further business there. Probably they could not endure the idea of remaining at the upper end of the lake while the battle between the two lines was going on at the other end. They had learned from our handbills, so profusely scattered through the town, that the Ucayga would make another through trip in the afternoon, and it was necessary for them to be at Ucayga to attend to the interests of the Lake Shore Railroad.

It was plain to me that Major Toppleton had come up to Hitaca with the warrant in his pocket, not to obtain justice for the injury which Tommy had sustained, but to interfere with the operations of the new line. I should have been arrested the day before if Grace Toppleton, whom I had come to regard as an angel of peace in my path, had not given me warning. My enemies must have been entirely satisfied that they could not hold me responsible for the damage done to Tommy, and my arrest was only intended as a blow at the steamboat line. At Hitaca, doubtless, they expected to detain my boat long enough, at least, to make her lose her connection at the lower end of the lake.

The arrival of the Ucayga at Hitaca, and the announcement of a new daily line, at reduced rates, had created no little excitement in the town. The people believed that they were to be better accommodated, and, very naturally, their sympathies were with the new line, as the large number of passengers we carried fully proved. The constable told me that he had been called upon to serve the warrant only a few minutes before he made his appearance on the wharf. He saw at once that it was a trick to annoy the new line, but he could not help himself. The moment Colonel Wimpleton showed him how he could discharge his duty without injury to the enterprise, he promptly embraced the opportunity. Major Toppleton and Tommy were doubtless sorely vexed at their failure; but they went into the cabin, and I did not see them again for some time.

It was a beautiful autumnal morning when the Ucayga started upon her trip, crowded with passengers. Colonel Wimpleton, alive to the importance of this day's work, had engaged the Hitaca Cornet Band to enliven the passage with their music. The weather was warm, and the soft haze of the Indian summer hung over the hills on the shore, where the woods presented the many hues of the changing foliage. The water was as tranquil as a dream of peace, and the inspiring strains of the band completed the pleasure of the occasion.

I explained to Colonel Wimpleton, Waddie, and others who were interested in the matter, the occasion of the proceedings against me. It is needless to say that I had no lack of friends; and, with the consent of the constable, it was arranged that he should take me before the magistrate at noon, while the boat was at Centreport. No charge could be proved against me, and I hardly gave the subject a thought.

The passage down the lake was a delightful one. We passed the old Ruoara just before we made the landing at Gulfport. At this town we saw Major Toppleton and his son go ashore, for the purpose of taking the railroad boat on her arrival. Neither of them showed himself on the trip, and I only hoped they appreciated the new steamer, and enjoyed the delightful music. I was rather afraid the colonel would court a collision with his powerful rival; but I am happy to say he was too good-natured, in the flush of his success, to exult over his enemy.

We made all our landings, and passing through the Horse Shoe Channel as usual, arrived at Ucayga on time. This concluded our first round trip to the head of the lake. It was a success far beyond our most sanguine hopes, and the exchequer of the Steamboat Company was largely benefited by it. The future was as bright as the present, and really I could not see that the Lake Shore Road had any chance against us.

But this was to be a day of excitement. Colonel Wimpleton landed at Centreport for the purpose of organizing a grand steamboat excursion to Ucayga and back in the afternoon; and when the boat returned I found the town in a blaze, for a pleasure trip, with a band of music, was no small affair to the people. Handbills were scattered throughout the place, and, as we had the advantage of a magnificent day, there was no want of enthusiasm on the subject.

As soon as the steamer reached Centreport, I went with the constable, Colonel Wimpleton, and the ablest

A TRICK OF THE ENEMY. Page 258.

lawyer in the place, over to Middleport. We found Captain Portman at the hotel, and hastened to the office of the magistrate. Like my friend from up the lake, I waived the examination, and was simply bound over to appear before the court several weeks hence for trial. Colonel Wimpleton and one of his friends gave bonds for my appearance, and the excitement in this direction was ended.

I went home, and invited my mother and sisters to the excursion in the afternoon. Of course I had a long story to tell of the history of the trip to Hitaca, and I had attentive listeners in the dear ones at home. I knew that my mother dreaded and deprecated the fearful rivalry which was going on between the two sides. I assured her that the best way to make peace was not always by giving up. One party was as nearly right as the other, and when each had shown his full strength there would be a better opportunity to heal the breach. I told her that, so far as I was concerned, and Waddie also, there was no ill feeling. It was a business competition, in which neither had any reason to complain of the other, so long as he did not trench upon his rights.

As I walked down to the lake with my mother and sisters, I saw Grace Toppleton in her father's garden. I wished that I could invite her to the excursion, for nothing could have added so much to its pleasure as her presence. But it was not proper for me to ask her, and it would not have been proper for her to accept if I had. I was proud and happy as I went on board of the Ucayga with my mother and sisters. The steamer was already filled with passengers, and at half past two we started. The band struck up an appropriate air as the wheels began to turn, and I never saw a happier party than that which crowded the decks of the Ucayga. In spite of the excitement, in spite of the throng on board, we were, as usual, on time.

When we touched the wharf near the railroad, the ferry-boat had arrived, and I saw Major Toppleton and Tommy on shore, listening to the music, and observing the multitude which covered our decks. I hoped I should not meet them, face to face, again; for I knew that our success had only increased their bitterness towards me. But they did not seem to be so ugly as when I had last seen them. Indeed, there was a smile upon their faces, as though the music delighted them. When our bow line was thrown ashore, they stepped on board, and came upon the hurricane deck, where I stood.

"You seem to be having a great time to-day, Wolf," said Tommy.

"Only a little excursion," I replied. "But the music is good, and I rather enjoy it."

"So do I, Wolf," answered Tommy, graciously. "I am going up with you, if you have no objection."

"Certainly not. Here is my state-room; and if you and your father will walk in, I will do the best I can to make you comfortable," I replied, pointing to my apartment.

"Thank you; I prefer to be on deck," added Tommy. "You have beaten us all to pieces to-day, Wolf, and we give it up now. What's the use of quarrelling about it?"

"None at all, most assuredly," I replied, with enthusiasm. "There is Waddie Wimpleton, who is just of your opinion."

"Well, I don't think much of Waddie, as you know, Wolf. I only meant that you and I wouldn't quarrel."

"I don't know why you and Waddie should quarrel. He intends to do the right thing."

"Perhaps he does; but the least said is soonest mended," said Tommy, rather coldly.

I was amazed and astounded at this sudden change of front in Tommy, who had hardly bestowed a pleasant word upon me for months. I could not feel sure that he meant what he said; but I resolved to afford him no cause of complaint if he really was sincere. It seemed to me more probable that he had some end to gain, under the mask of friendship, than that he was willing to make peace with me.

"Your boat appears to be doing remarkably well to-day, Wolf," said Major Toppleton, stepping up to me.

"Yes, sir; she is making good trips to-day."

"By the way, Wolf, you need give yourself no uneasiness about that trial. I caused your arrest under a misapprehension, and no harm shall come to you."

"I am very glad to hear you say so, sir, though I really had no fears of the consequences."

"I am going to adopt Tommy's suggestions, and have no more quarrelling," added the great man.

"I hope not, sir."

"You can have it all your own way on the lake now."

"I only wish to do what is right."

"I know you do, Wolf. Are you at home in the evening, now?"

"No, sir. I have to spend the night at Hitaca. I suppose our family will move up there soon, and you will get rid of us then."

"We don't desire to get rid of you," interposed Tommy.

"I want to see you, Wolf, when you are at leisure," continued the major. "When can you call upon me?"

"To-morrow noon, if you please," I replied, delighted at the prospect of again being permitted to stand under the same roof with Grace.

"I will be at home," said the magnate, as he walked away at the approach of Colonel Wimpleton.

CHAPTER XXVI.

MAJOR TOPPLETON'S PROPOSITION.

"WHAT does Toppleton want with you?" asked Colonel Wimpleton, coming up to me after the major and his son had retired.

The magnate of Centreport looked ugly, as though, in the moment of his great triumph, he feared a conspiracy to rob the Steamboat Company of the laurels it had won.

" Nothing in particular, that I am aware of," I replied, not exactly pleased to have even an unkind look bestowed upon me, after the victory which I had been instrumental in winning.

" You seem to be on excellent terms with him," sneered the colonel.

" I do not wish to quarrel with any one."

" What did Toppleton want?" demanded the great man, rather more sharply than the occasion seemed to require.

"I don't know that he wants anything. He invited me to call at his house, and I promised to do so," I answered, candidly.

"You did!"

"I did, sir. Both the major and Tommy were kind enough to say that they did not wish to quarrel with me; and certainly I have no ill will against them."

"You have not!" repeated Colonel Wimpleton, with emphasis. "Am I not your bail on a groundless charge preferred by them?"

"But they have done me more of good than of evil; and the major said no harm should come to me on account of the trial."

"Wolf, I don't like this way of doing things. If you are in my service, I don't want you to have anything to do with my enemies. If three dollars a day is not enough for a boy like you, I will give you four or five; but you mustn't play into the hands of Toppleton."

"I don't intend to do so, sir. I never yet deserted those who used me well, and I don't intend to begin now. If you think you cannot trust me, sir, don't do it."

The time for starting having arrived, the conversation, which did not promise very agreeable results, was interrupted. The band struck up its music, and the Ucayga left the wharf. I went into my state-room for the purpose of being alone a moment, for I wanted to think over what the colonel had just said to me. He was evidently jealous of anything like intimacy between the Toppletons and myself, and was afraid I would "sell out" the Steamboat Company. I was not flattered by the suspicion. I considered the subject very faithfully; but I decided that it was unreasonable in my present patron to insist that I should have nothing to do with the Toppletons. As long as Grace lived and smiled upon me, I could assent to nothing of the kind, even if I lost my situation. At the same time, I intended to be true to my employers, even if Grace ceased to smile upon me for doing so.

On the up trip the Ucayga was even uncomfortably crowded; for, besides the excursion party, we had a large number of through passengers. But, as soon as the boat was clear of the wharf, they began to settle down, and to cease to crowd each other. The band played splendidly, and everybody seemed to be satisfied. At Centreport we left the crowd, though the

boat was still well filled. The programme of the pre-
ceding day was repeated. We passed the old Ruoara
near Gulfport, and arrived at Hitaca a little before the
time in my table. As we had kept all our promises,
the new line was in high favor with the public.

The next morning, the old boat departed with hardly a corporal's guard of passengers, while the Ucayga
was crowded. We landed our freight at Ucayga on
time, and everybody was satisfied that the new line
was an assured success. I need not follow its triumphs
any farther, for it would be only a repetition of what
has already been said. The steamboat line was carrying nearly all the passengers. The old-line boats had
hardly business enough to pay for the oil used on the
machinery, though the Lake Shore Railroad did tolerably well with its local trade.

When the Ucayga arrived at Centreport, on the day
after the excursion, I crossed the lake ; and, after a
short visit to my mother, I hastened to the mansion of
Major Toppleton. I did not stay to dine, as I usually
did when I went home, for my time was limited, and I
could obtain my noonday meal on board the steamer
after my return. I was not only curious to know what

18

the major wanted of me, but I was thirsting for the opportunity to meet Grace. The latter motive was doubtless the stronger one ; for, since the poor girl had risked so much to give me warning of the intended arrest, I flattered myself that she was not wholly indifferent to me.

With a fluttering heart I rang the bell at the door of Major Toppleton's house. I was admitted to the library. Neither the great man nor his son was at home ; but the servant assured me they would soon return, for it wanted but a few minutes of lunch time. I ventured to ask if Miss Grace was at home. I knew she was, for I heard the piano in one of the neighboring rooms, and the music was so sweet I was sure no mortal hands but hers could produce it. In a moment she entered the library, her soft cheeks crimsoned with a blush, which made me feel exceedingly awkward.

" Why, Mr. Wolf! I am so glad to see you ! " said she ; and, in the enthusiasm of the moment, she advanced towards me, and gave me her little hand.

" I'm sure you cannot be as glad to see me as I am to see you," I replied, pressing the little hand in mine.

Dear me! What was I doing? Straightway I began to feel very queer and awkward, and cheap and mean. She was confused, and apparently astonished by the boldness of my remark, for she retired to a sofa on the other side of the room. I was beginning to thank her for the great service she had rendered me on Monday, when Major Toppleton and Tommy, whom the stupid servant had taken the trouble to summon, entered the library. I wished they had deferred their coming for half an hour. Both of them seemed to be very glad to see me, and took no notice of the presence of Grace. To my astonishment, the magnate invited me to lunch with him. I had not the courage to refuse, or, in other words, to banish myself from the presence of Grace.

" Wolf, we had just nine passengers from Hitaca this morning," said the major, with a chuckling laugh, as though he intended to make the best of his discomfiture.

" We had over two hundred and fifty," I replied.

" Yesterday afternoon we had a fair freight down ; but we can't do anything against that new steamer, especially when you have a band of music on board," added the major. "Will you take some of this cold chicken?"

"Thank you, sir — a little. For your sake I am sorry the steamboat line is doing so well."

"You can do anything you please with Colonel Wimpleton, just now," he added.

"I think not, sir."

"I believe you can. The fact is, you suggested the plan by which the railroad line has been defeated."

"But the plan is already in working order, and it will go on just as well without me as with me."

"I am sorry we had any trouble with you, Wolf, for suddenly from a boy you have become a man, and a dangerous man, too, for our side of the lake."

I was forced to believe that this was mere flattery, intended to help along some object not yet mentioned.

"I have done the best I could for my employers, on whichever side I happened to be engaged."

"That's true. I am going to speak plainly now, Wolf. We are beaten; but we don't intend to remain beaten for any great length of time. The prosperity of Middleport depends greatly upon the Lake Shore Railroad, and I intend to make that a success if it costs me all I am worth. I shall build a bridge at the foot of the lake, so that I can go into Ucayga with. out the aid of a ferry-boat. A Lightning Express is going through from Middleport to the station at Ucay. ga in three quarters of an hour. So far I am determined."

"That will not help your case much, so far as through travel is concerned."

"Considerable, Wolf. We shall save fifteen minutes."

"But we shall still beat you by half an hour."

"Very true; but I don't intend to stop here. I shall either build a steamer equal or superior to the Ucayga, to run between Hitaca and Middleport, or I shall run the railroad to the head of the lake."

"Will it pay?"

"I think it will; but, though Wimpleton and I have always quarrelled of late years, I am willing to be fair. I have a plan, which I will state to you. If Wimpleton will run the Ucayga from Hitaca to Middleport in connection with the railroad, I will take off my boats. This will be a fair thing for both of us. You may

state the case to him. If he agrees to it, all right; if
not, I shall make my next move."

This, then, was what the major was driving at, and I
was to be the ambassador between the rivals. I was
willing to do the best I could, but I proposed that
Tommy and Waddie should meet and discuss the matter. The little magnate of Middleport promptly and
indignantly refused to meet the other little magnate.
I promised to report the next day on my mission. As
I was leaving, I invited Mrs. Toppleton and Grace to
make a trip with me up or down the lake. Somewhat
to my surprise, at the suggestion of the major, they
accepted the invitation for that day. We crossed the
lake, and I assure the reader I took every pains to
make my guests happy.

Neither Waddie nor his father was on board again
that day; but the latter went up to Hitaca with me
in the afternoon. Cautiously approaching the subject,
I stated Major Toppleton's proposition. The colonel
would hardly listen to it, much less accept it. He
swore, and abused his great rival. He would have
nothing to do with Toppleton. He would sink the
Ucayga before he would help the railroad to a single

passenger. He was very savage, and, before he had finished, poured out the vials of his wrath upon me for mentioning the subject.

The next day I reported the result of my mission; and Major Toppleton was quite as savage as the colonel had been. He swore, too, and declared that he would run the Ucayga off the route before another summer.

I spoke to Waddie on the subject, and he expressed a strong desire to meet Tommy, and to be friends with him. He favored the plan of Major Toppleton, and if he had possessed as much influence over his father as Tommy over his, the arrangement would doubtless have been made. I was not without hope that the plan might yet be adopted.

But I have told my story as a steamboat captain; and anything more would be but a repetition. I had labored to make peace, but had failed. If there were olive branches in the future, there were none in the present. I continued to run the Ucayga during the winter, with the same success which attended her from the first of my connection with her. We did about all the through business, and the Lake Shore Railroad languished under the competition.

At the next meeting of the Steamboat Company Waddie resigned, to the intense indignation of his father, and Dick Bayard was elected president. He also declined a reëlection as major of the battalion, and Ben Pinkerton was chosen to the command. Thus far Waddie was true to his good resolutions, though he had much difficulty with his father on account of the change. He often came to me for advice, for the students of the Institute seemed to distrust him still. No mutiny or rebellion occurred on his side of the lake, for the resigning of his offices prevented any collision.

Tom Walton made a good thing out of the Belle, and when the season closed, I obtained a place for him as deck hand on board of the Ucayga, where he did tolerably well for the winter.

In November our family moved up to Hitaca, for my father and I were compelled to spend our nights and Sundays at that port. Our place in Middleport was let for the winter. Occasionally, while lying at Centreport, I made an errand over to Major Toppleton's that I might see Grace; but I seldom met her. I hoped, most earnestly, that the two lines might be united, and peace restored between the two great houses. As Waddie was in favor of it, the prospect was not altogether dark. As the union meant peace, I continued to labor for it. If effected, the Ucayga would lie at the wharf in Middleport between trips. I earnestly desired it. Then Grace would be a frequent passenger on the boat.

I have told the story of "The Young Captain of the Ucayga Steamer;" how he became captain, and how well he succeeded in this capacity. The story is complete, and nothing more remains to be said of him; but the history of the great quarrel between the two sides of the lake, which has other phases, is not finished. There is another story to be told; but, as most of its events transpired while I was absent, I could only tell it from hearsay. I prefer that it should be related by an actual witness; and for this reason I have invited my friend Ned Skotchley to take the pen, and write "SWITCH OFF; OR, THE WAR OF THE STUDENTS."

I told Ned not to say anything more about me than ue was obliged to do; but he is an obstinate fellow, and I find, by looking over his manuscript, that he has, to a very great extent, disregarded my instructions. But I am not responsible for the praise he bestows upon me, though, whatever he says of me, I am conscious that I have tried to be a Christian, to be faithful to my employers, and always to be " ON TIME."

WOODVILLE STORIES.

Uniform with Library for Young People. Six vols. 16mo. Illustrated. Per vol., $1.25.

1. **RICH AND HUMBLE;**
   Or, The Mission of Bertha Grant.

2. **IN SCHOOL AND OUT;**
   Or, The Conquest of Richard Grant.

3. **WATCH AND WAIT;**
   Or, The Young Fugitives.

4. **WORK AND WIN;**
   Or, Noddy Newman on a Cruise.

5. **HOPE AND HAVE;**
   Or, Fanny Grant among the Indians.

6. **HASTE AND WASTE;**
   Or, The Young Pilot of Lake Champlain.

Though we are not so young as we once were, we relished these stories almost as much as the boys and girls for whom they were written. They were really refreshing even to us. There is much in them which is calculated to inspire a generous, healthy ambition, and to make distasteful all reading tending to stimulate base desires. — *Fitchburg Reveille.*

THE ONWARD AND UPWARD

SERIES.

**Complete in six volumes. Illustrated. In neat box.
Per volume, $1.25.**

1. FIELD AND FOREST;
Or, The Fortunes of a Farmer.

2. PLANE AND PLANK;
Or, The Mishaps of a Mechanic.

3. DESK AND DEBIT;
Or, The Catastrophes of a Clerk.

4. CRINGLE AND CROSS-TREE;
Or, The Sea Swashes of a Sailor.

5. BIVOUAC AND BATTLE;
Or, The Struggles of a Soldier.

6. SEA AND SHORE;
Or, The Tramps of a Traveller.

Paul Farringford, the hero of these tales, is, like most of this author's heroes, a young man of high spirit, and of high aims and correct principles, appearing in the different volumes as a farmer, a captain, a bookkeeper, a soldier, a sailor, and a traveller. In all of them the hero meets with very exciting adventures, told in the graphic style for which the author is famous. — *Native.*

www.ingramcontent.com/pod-product-compliance
Lightning Source LLC
Chambersburg PA
CBHW060600030726
47498CB00005B/1469